christine Li

Armstrong

P9-CQI-701

Orphan
at My Door

The Home Child Diary
of Victoria Cope

BY JEAN LITTLE

Scholastic Canada Ltd.

Guelph, Ontario,
1897

This diary belongs to:
Victoria Josephine Cope,
264 Woolwich St.,
Town of Guelph,
Province of Ontario,
Dominion of Canada.

May

Monday, May 24, 1897, 10 in the morning

The 24th of May
Is the Queen's birthday.
If we don't get a holiday,
We'll all run away.

But we *did* get a holiday from school. We always do. And, because I was born on May 24, I always get a holiday on MY birthday too. This morning, I turned eleven and Queen Victoria turned seventy-eight. Happy birthday to her majesty and to me, her majesty's namesake and loyal subject, Victoria Josephine Cope.

Next month we are going to be celebrating the diamond jubilee of her reign. She was crowned sixty years ago, when she was eighteen. Mother always says, "only eighteen," as though she were a baby of five or six. But I think eighteen is plenty old enough to be a queen.

I have to go, but I could not wait to write something in my brand new birthday diary. I wonder if I should call it "Dear Diary" and talk to it as though it is a person. I'll have to try that and see how it feels. I've never kept a diary before, not an important one with a ribbon to mark my place.

I'll be back as soon as I can, dear Diary. It is hard to get time to yourself if you are a girl. Tom and David have definite chores and, once they have finished them, their time is their own. But housework you never finish. My Grandma Sinclair used to say, "A man can work from sun to sun, But woman's work is never done."

It is too true.

Still my birthday, Early afternoon

Mother has fallen asleep. It is strange. She never used to lie down in the daytime, but lately, whenever I am not at school, I have noticed her taking a nap right after the noon dishes are done. I thought only babies and old people slept in the afternoon. When Mother is asleep, the house feels empty somehow.

It is really far from empty though. The boys are out with their friends, but Father is in his office, and I can hear Peggy's footsteps tramping back and forth in her room at the end of the hall. I wonder what's wrong with her. She is not singing. She usually sings "Annie Laurie" or some other sad song over and over until you want to scream at her to stop. You should hear her do "Last Rose of Summer," Diary, and you'd fully sympathize with my feelings. Whenever Tom and I complain to Mother, she tells us not to ruffle Peggy's feathers. "She's a good-hearted, hard-working girl and they are not easy to come by," she says.

But never mind Peggy. At this very moment, nobody in the world knows where I am or what I'm doing. I feel as though I have been given a birthday present of some time which is my very own.

So, dear Diary, I came straight to you.

When I grow up, I want to write books like Louisa May Alcott. After all, I'm named Josephine after Jo March in *Little Women* and my Grandma Cope. Jo is Mother's favourite character, although Mother seems much more like Meg to me. When I told her that, she smiled a little and said, "I'm still Jo inside, Victoria. But would you really want a mother who kept jumping fences?" Maybe I would.

I will start by describing my family. Writers have to describe people all the time. It will be good practice for me.

My father, Alastair John Cope, is a doctor who wants to make the world better for poor people. It is a good thing rich people like him too, or we might be poor ourselves. He is tall and quite handsome. His eyes are hazel like mine and his hair is the same sandy brown as mine. So is his moustache, although it has some grey mixed in. He is kind but he does like to tease a little too much.

His office is in our house. There's a side door and a sign saying: Dr. ALASTAIR COPE, M.D., Physician and Surgeon.

My mother's name is Lilias Jemima Cope and she looks after us all. She has hair exactly the colour of our dining room table. I think it's mahogany. Her eyes are forget-me-not blue. She is serious and stately, although she does have a sense of fun. I heard Father say once that she was like a tall sailing ship, and he was right.

Moses, our tabby cat, just jumped up to see what I'm doing. So I'll tell about her next. Her name is Moses because my brother Tom found her in the river. Someone had tried to drown her, but she was clinging to an old apple basket. He fished her out, put her in the basket and brought her home to Mother. Everyone loves Moses, although she is no mouser. Everyone also thinks that Moses is a strange name for a girl, but since she was saved from drowning and brought ashore in a basket, like the Baby Moses in the Bible, it seemed the only name possible.

So now, back to the rest of my family. I have two older brothers, David and Thomas. I had another one, Douglas Alastair, but he died before I was born. He only lived three days. He was Mother and Father's first child and, even though we don't talk about him, Mother always puts a tiny bunch of flowers on his marker when we go to the graveyard on Sundays. On his stone there is just his name and the words "With God."

I wonder what Heaven is really like and what happens to babies who go there. There are so many of them buried in the graveyard. Their little stones have brought tears to my eyes. They died before they even knew who they were. I can't understand how God lets it happen, but Father says even God must obey the laws of Nature.

David is sixteen and in high school. He is supposed to be highly intelligent because he likes to play chess and he wins prizes in Mathematics. It is too bad somebody told him how clever he is because it went to his head. He thinks he's better than the rest of us. He treats Tom and me as though we were babies.

David gave me plaid hair ribbons for my birthday, but I overheard Mother telling him she'd bought them for him to give to me. "Vic won't expect a present from me," he'd said. He was right about that.

"Well, she's getting one," Mother told him. "You sign this card, young man, and I'll do the rest."

He did what she said, but when he left, he banged the door behind him. I got the ribbons and card at breakfast, and thanked him with a molasses sweet smile. He nodded but could not look me in the eye.

Tom says David has made friends with some rich boys and they are turning him into a snob. Mother is worried about this, but Father says to give him time and he'll come to his senses. It sounds a bit like, "Give him enough rope and he'll hang himself." Father says that about people sometimes. I'm not sure what he means by it.

Maybe I shouldn't talk about David that way, but I promised myself to be honest in this diary. The truth is, I love David but I don't like him much. I used to think he was wonderful. I remember his teaching me to play scissors, paper, stone. Then he found out how highly intelligent he was and he had no more time for little sisters.

Thomas — I usually call him Tom but Mother and Father call him Thomas — is almost fourteen and just finishing his Entrance. He and I are good friends most of the time, and if I get in trouble, he always stands up for me. He gave me a book for my birthday — he picked it out himself — and bought it with his own money. He found it in the secondhand stall in front of the bookstore. It is *The Water Babies* by Charles Kingsley, and it looks wonderful. I started reading it right after breakfast and it is terribly sad. Tom knows I love sad books. It is all about a little chimney sweep, also called Tom, who has a cruel master. It is hard to believe anyone could be so unkind to a little boy. I have not read all that much and I have cried buckets already.

This morning, before breakfast, Mother gave me this diary. It is the first book I have ever had with a ribbon to mark my place. She said I am to write in it every day, if possible, and that if I miss a day or two, just to start in again and don't feel that I have to fill in everything that happened since last time.

"Too many people give up keeping a journal once they miss a few days," she said. "Promise me you'll keep going."

I promised.

Then she said, "No embroidery, Victoria. Just write down what really happens each day. When you grow up, you will love having the true story of your twelfth year."

I wanted to ask her why she does so much embroidery herself if she hates it. Our pillowcases are stiff with her roses and pansies and violets. But I didn't.

I dearly love making up stories. When my Great-Aunt Lib visits and catches me telling one, she calls them lies. Mother calls them "falsehoods," but I don't understand why. Jo March certainly likes making up stories, and Mother loves Jo. But she is forever telling me that detestable fable about the boy who cried wolf. I abominate that boy. Stories are not the same as lies.

Since I plan to become a writer, I'll put in lots of talking. I hate books where there are whole pages without anyone saying a word. I also like listening. Writers have to be able to make the talking sound real or the book is no good.

For my birthday Father gave me a little writing desk I can put across my lap when I sit in bed and write in my diary. It is a shallow wooden box with a lid, so you can keep your pens and blotter inside. It has the sweetest little inkpot that fits into a hole in one corner. Father says he thinks Jane Austen had one like it.

I had better stop for now. My hand is aching and I am making ink blots. I'll be back, Diary.

Still my birthday, After supper

Here I am again, dear Diary. Moses is sitting next to me watching to see what I am up to. She wants to play with my pen.

We had Burnt Leather Cake for dessert, in honour of my birthday. I used to be fascinated by it because it had such a strange name, but now I just plain like the taste of it. Everybody else likes devil's food cake better.

Peggy came in to eat her cake with us. She got the wedding ring in her piece of cake, and when she saw it she burst into tears. Why? It isn't as though she has no beau. She's sweet on the blacksmith's apprentice, Joseph Connor. If she'd found the thimble, like me, she would have had something to cry about. The thimble means you are going to be an old maid and sew on hundreds of buttons. Something like that.

Everyone laughed when they saw that thimble. I suppose it was because my sewing is so lumpy and bumpy. Bloodstained too. I'm worse than Snow White's mother.

When I was a baby, Mother embroidered a sampler to put on my bedroom wall. It says:

Be good, sweet maid, and let who can be clever.
Do noble things, not dream them all day long.

I have not told Mother, but I confess here that I would rather be clever than a goody goody sweet maid. I've been told many times how overjoyed Mother was when she at last had a baby daughter. She probably thought I would like ruffles and ribbons and be dainty and pretty. What a sad disappointment I must have been!

"If I write the truth in my diary, are you going to read what I put down?" I asked Mother. It was going to be a dull book if she said yes.

She laughed. "No, Victoria," she said. "Diaries are private. But I want you to do your best to tell the truth anyway. You dream of becoming a writer. But writers have to make the truth interesting, you know."

I did not know she guessed I dream of becoming a writer some day.

She's calling. She's saying I forgot to put the dishes away. I did NOT forget. I thought Peggy would do it since it's my birthday. I'll be back soon, Diary.

Bedtime

Dr. Graham, who is Mother's doctor, came by today. (Doctors are not supposed to treat their own families. Father looks after the little daily things like our cuts and scrapes, but Dr. Graham takes care of us if we get really sick.) I asked Mother if she were ill, because he seems to come over far more often lately. She said she was fine, just a bit tired. I can't think why she would be especially tired. Yet I heard Dr. G. tell Father she needs more help in the house.

Father said something about finding someone to come in daily to give a hand with the heavy work. I was surprised, because Peggy is a good worker. I've heard Mother say so. She could do the heavy work.

Then Father said Mother was going to be upset when she learned about Peggy.

Learned what about Peggy? I knew better than to ask, so I stayed still and strained my ears.

"I'm going to Peterborough tomorrow to attend a family shindig," Dr. Graham said. "Why don't I go to Hazelbrae for you and ask them to let you have a Home Girl? She'd live in. Write a note appointing me your deputy, and there shouldn't be any trouble. They know me."

What did he mean about Peggy? I could not ask because I was eavesdropping. I'd have had to listen to the same old lecture I get every time they catch me listening. I am certain Louisa May Alcott eavesdropped.

I wonder what those Home Girls are like. I've always wanted a sister, but I suppose they are nothing like us. Orphanages send them here to rescue them from the terrible slums in London. They are like the pickpocket boys in *Oliver Twist*, I suppose. Or like the little match girl.

If I write this much every day I will have filled this diary before Christmas. It's a good thing Mother found a really fat diary for me. Even if I had not much to say, my penmanship is not small and neat. Ask Mr.

Grigson. He's always shaking his head over my copy-book.

I am getting another present from Mother and Father tomorrow. They seem excited about it, but they won't even give me a hint about what it is. Tom says it is a catechism book. He is as bad as Father when it comes to teasing.

Just before I came up to bed, Father asked me what I thought of the world. "Now you are eleven and entering upon your twelfth year, you are old enough to think about such things," he said.

I think he was teasing, but I told him the truth. "It is a wonderful world," I said. "And it is a special year to be eleven. A jubilee year."

"Promise me you will do your best to stay jubilant, Victoria," he said, looking serious, "whatever troubles this old world has in store for us."

"I promise," I said.

What troubles was he talking about, dear Diary? Never mind. I promised. And now my hand is cramping from so much writing.

Tuesday, May 25, After supper

My special present came this morning and made me late for school. Mother wrote me a note to explain, and Tom and I ran most of the way there. I was so excited all day I could not keep my mind on my studies.

Uncle Peter delivered it. His wife, my Auntie Gwen, has a pug dog called Clover. She had three puppies, and Mother and Father got me one of them! ("Because Queen Victoria has one," Father said.)

He is perfect. His kennel name is Prince Rudolph, but that sounds silly. I'll think up a name that exactly suits him. He is very young and keeps making puddles on the floor. He is apricot-coloured with a tightly curled tail and a black mask. I can hold him in my two cupped hands, although he will be about fourteen pounds when he grows up. He has the pinkest scrap of a tongue you have ever seen. His little face is wrinkled and his little ears feel like velvet.

I keep him with me all the time, except when he is sleeping. He is sound asleep now, so I can write all about the BIG NEWS. Puppies sleep a lot.

At noon Mother told us that Peggy has left us. She gave notice after I went to bed last night, and this morning she packed and departed without saying goodbye.

When I came home from school, it was strange not to find her here. Mother said she is getting married. She is only fifteen! She was crying at breakfast and she hardly seemed to notice my puppy. No wonder!

I looked into her room tonight. It is so bare and empty. I started to ask if I could go to the wedding, but Mother said no. When I began to ask why not, she said she did not want to talk about it. I guess she thinks Peggy is too young.

I wish I knew why the thought of getting married made Peggy, who is usually cheerful, keep crying. I won't marry somebody who makes me cry. Maybe she was sad to be leaving us, but I don't think so. She has not been with us that long. She was just turned fourteen when she came.

"Forget Peggy for the moment," Father said at supper when I tried questioning him. "I have an announcement. I've already sent off a letter with Douglas Graham to Hazelbrac — that's the Barnardo place in Peterborough — asking for a Home Girl. Now all we need do is find a woman to come in daily to help with the heavier work, and we'll be set."

Mother said that wasn't necessary, but she did not sound as though she meant it. She looked tired and worried.

You might not think I remember exactly what they said, dear Diary, but I do. Oh, I might have a word or phrase wrong, but I was enthralled. If only Father hadn't made Mother hush up about Peggy. But Peggy's gone, so I'll give up wondering about her and think about this Home Girl.

While we ate, my poor puppy was shut out in the kitchen. I could hear him crying at first, and after the talk turned to ordinary things I had trouble paying attention to what people were saying. But he fell asleep before too long.

"That pup certainly is a homely little thing," Mother said.

"Gwen says the uglier they are the better bred they are," Father reminded her with a laugh. "Prince Rudolph must be the best bred pug in the country, right, Vic?"

I looked daggers at him and scorned to answer.

Now Mother is calling me to come down and set the table for breakfast. I hope we get a new maid soon. When Billy Grant comes in for his morning cup of tea, he just sits and waits for someone to fetch it for him. Billy Grant is the old man who looks after everything outside, including cutting the grass, mending the shutters, cleaning out the eavestroughs and taking care of Father's horse, Bess. He polishes up the buggy and the Family Conveyance too. That's what we call the carriage. He lives alone in a little cottage on London Road and he hardly speaks. Now, when I am home, I have to fetch Billy's tea for him. He is old, so I can see someone should wait on him. But I am sure he would have sat and waited the same way if he had been twenty.

Bedtime

When they sent me to bed, I had to leave my poor pup behind. He is in a big lidded basket in the back kitchen. Mother said it would be unhealthy to have a dog in my bed and that he'd sleep like a top in the basket. Father backed her up.

"If he were sleeping in your bed, Victoria, you

would be swimming by morning."

They don't understand. Every time I open my bedroom door a crack, I can hear them laughing and playing with MY puppy. I plan to keep listening until I hear not a sound down there. When they are asleep, I will go down and make sure he is all right.

And while I'm waiting to sneak downstairs I'll describe myself, since when I read over my diary just now I realized that I forgot to tell about me yesterday.

I have sandy brown braids which hang down my back, hazel eyes with greenish specks, skin that has faint freckles even in winter, and a wide thin mouth. My hands are beautiful. My Grandmother Sinclair said so before she died. She said they were "the hands of a musician." They are long and slender. But nobody notices them now Grandma is gone.

My Great-Aunt Lib told me my mouth is far too big for a girl, but she says mean things about everybody. She even says Mother spoils us and "can't handle servants." Aunt Lib is Mother's aunt and my Grandma Sinclair's big sister. It is strange how Grandma was so kind and her sister is the exact opposite.

I also forgot to say I have dimples. People tease me about them but I like them, because Mother has them too, in exactly the same places.

In the wee small hours

I did it!

Staying awake was hard, but I kept pinching myself. It was simple to creep down the back stairs without anyone hearing me. My darling was crying his heart out. I petted him but then could not leave him alone again, however nice the basket is. He is now in bed with me. I have put two thick towels under him. I wonder if Mother heard me. Father didn't. He snored the whole time.

I guess it isn't really "the wee small hours" because the clock just struck midnight. The wee ones must be one and two and maybe three. But I like the sound of "wee small hours."

Wednesday, May 26

I only had to take the puppy out once, just before sunrise. He did not wet my bed. He snuggled up to me all night. I thought I might call him Snuggle, but decided that sounds too soft for a boy dog.

Mother has doubts about getting a Home Girl. It came up at breakfast.

She told Father she'd heard that some of them were rough street children, waifs and strays. "What if the girl they send is a sly minx who has stolen from the cradle up?" she asked. "We have to protect our own children."

"Lilias, I am speaking of a girl. Some of the boys may

be ruffians. Those I've met have been just lads out of luck. Surely girls are born ladies. Look at our Victoria — a lady to her fingertips."

I giggled. Tom grinned. David didn't even smile. Now he's in Fourth Form, he finds the rest of us embarrassing.

"Why don't we get a proper maid?" he said. "Nathan's father says Home Children are diseased and feeble-minded and unfit to be with Canadian young people." Then he told father he had a position to keep up. He sounded so snooty and pompous.

Father looked at him and said coolly, "I know Nathan's father. He has many opinions with which I heartily disagree. Please, David, do not swallow what he tells you without thinking for yourself. Also remember what our Lord Jesus commanded us to do: Feed the hungry, clothe the naked, visit the prisoner. He did not once mention keeping up your position."

Maybe I have not got every word right, but that is more or less what he said. I felt as though his words were burned into my brain. David went red and stared hard at the calendar hanging on the wall. Father had shamed him, but I don't think he changed his mind about our getting a Home Girl.

Mother and Father talked on a little longer but, of course, Mother gave in at last.

"When the girl arrives, perhaps I should take Victoria with me to meet her," Father said all at once. "She could make sure I brought home one who would suit you, and the girl might be nervous going off alone with a stranger."

Mother said that was a good notion.

I do hope whoever we get is nicer than Peggy and does not poke fun at my freckles. I also got tired of listening to her sing "Annie Laurie." Tom always said she sang like a cow in agony. Her voice wobbled too. She thought it was what great singers did.

Moses will miss the tidbits Peggy always saved for her. Oh, I will miss her too. You get used to people being around in your life. I wonder if she will miss us.

We had Aunt Janet's gingerbread with whipped cream and fresh applesauce for dessert tonight. Mmmm! Tom had three pieces. He asked for another but Mother said she had to draw the line somewhere.

"But, Mother, I'm a growing boy," Tom pleaded.

"That's what worries me," Mother said and put the gingerbread away. She always saves a couple of big pieces for Billy Grant. He says it tastes just like his mother's used to. It is hard to imagine Billy Grant with a mother. His face always reminds me of a walnut.

Bedtime, Thursday, May 27

I almost forgot to write in this book tonight. I can't write much because Mother called up to me to blow out my candle.

I blew it out, but I went on reading by the light

from the window. I am halfway through *The Water Babies* and I am in the middle of a very exciting part. Putting it down at that moment would have been torture. It is dusk now though. So I stopped while I could see well enough to write.

My puppy just made a funny little grunting snort. Maybe Snortle would do for a name. Snortle keeps trying to eat the elbow of my nightgown where there is a ruffle with a ribbon threaded through it. A puppy is a lot of work.

He knows his name! I said, "Hello, Snortle," and he raised his head and looked right at me. Clever Snortle!

Mother made me cart his basket up here but she also put a rubber sheet on the bed.

"If you are going to feel compelled to creep through the house in the dead of night to check up on his welfare, I will never get a wink of sleep." She sighed. "We had better give in first as last and let you take him upstairs."

She also said that if he makes a mess, I am responsible for cleaning it up.

"Yes, ma'am," I said meekly and bobbed her a curtsy.

That made her smile.

I hate the rubber sheet. It feels hard and it crackles whenever I move the least bit. Snortle does not seem to mind, but Moses jumped up once, and the second she heard the noise it makes and felt its stiffness, she leapt down and stalked out of the room, tail tall with disgust. When I am a mother, I will never put a rubber sheet on a child's bed.

I will also let my children read in bed until they fall asleep.

Snortle makes concentrating on a book more difficult, but he is worth it.

I am choosing a piece to say at the school closing exercises. I thought I might learn "Little Boy Blue" by Eugene Field. It's all about a little boy dying, and his toys waiting for him to come back to them. But Father says no daughter of his will stand up in public and recite such sentimental drivel. I thought it was beautiful before he said that. It brought tears to my eyes. Now it sounds a bit silly. Maybe I'll do "The Charge of the Light Brigade" instead. You could do wonderful gestures.

Bedtime, Friday, May 28

Alas, alack and woe is me! Mother told us at supper that Great-Aunt Lib and Cousin Anna are coming to visit! They are AWFUL! Mother lived with Aunt Lib on weekdays while she went to high school in Guelph for three years. Her parents' farm was too far out in the country for her to drive in every day. She feels she owes Aunt Lib gratitude.

That is all very well. But when Aunt Lib visits our house, she is painful to have around, and not only Mother suffers but all of us. Father seems to go on more house calls and he makes more appointments in the evening, which keep him safely shut behind his office door. David and Tom go to their room to do their homework instead of doing it at the kitchen table the way they do when Aunt Lib is not here.

"Tell her we can't have her," David said. "You don't have to lie. Just say that . . . that we are moving to Winnipeg. I can't bring anyone over while they are in the house."

I thought it was a good idea. Not the part about Winnipeg, but just saying we can't have them visit right now. But Mother stared at him helplessly.

Father said in a dry voice, "They are already on their way, aren't they, dear Lilias? That's what they did last time, remember?"

"Yes, but still, David should not speak of them that way. None of their problems are their fault."

Then she told me I would have to keep "Prince Rudolph" out from under their feet or we'll end up with Aunt Lib tripping over him and breaking her leg.

"Prince Rudolph is not my puppy's name. It does not fit him. I've named him Snortle," I said. "He makes a sort of snuffling snort — "

"That's a perfect name for him," Mother said.

"That's a perfect name for Aunt Lib," Tom laughed. "She's always snorting at things."

I'd have been scolded, but they laughed at Tom. I don't understand why boys get away with things girls don't.

Suddenly I saw Mother looking tired out. I don't remember her ever looking like that before. Lately she has dark circles under her eyes and she sighs a lot. She is taking a tonic though. Burdock Blood Bitters. Her friend, Mrs. Spence, said it really perked her up. Maybe it will help Mother too.

Father said it was hogwash. Then he himself gave her some iron extract and cod liver oil. She makes terrible faces when she gulps them down.

Father suggested that we put a Smallpox sign on the door since Cousin Anna is a dyed-in-the-wool hypochondriac. I asked him what that meant and how to spell it and he made me look it up in the dictionary. Mother shook her head at him but his eyes glinted with laughter. (Glinted is a good word too. Louisa May Alcott used words like that.)

"Poor things," Mother said. "Nobody wants them and I doubt they have money to spare."

"I'm not so sure they are as hard up as you think," Father said. Then he changed the subject fast, asking if she had found someone to take Peggy's place.

She had! Mrs. Cameron from next door knew a woman who had been left a widow with a crippled son to raise. Her name is Mrs. Dougal and she is coming over to meet Mother tomorrow.

"Did you tell her about the upcoming Event . . . ?" Father asked, lowering his voice. I think he thought I would not hear him.

"Yes. I told her everything," Mother said.

I was about to ask what they meant, but I could not pay attention because of dreading Aunt Lib's visit. I am plunged in gloom. Last time, she and Cousin Anna stayed six weeks. Mother says Aunt Lib has "a good heart." Father says that when Mother tells us someone has a good heart, watch out. It means there is nothing else good about her. I think he hit the nail on the head.

We had lemon snow pudding with custard sauce for dessert. I like the pudding all right. It is wonderfully fluffy. But I LOVE Mother's custard sauce. It is so rich and smooth. I could drink the whole pitcher full.

Billy Grant likes lemon snow pudding too. But he won't come into the kitchen for a cup of tea if Aunt Lib is in the house. One of us has to take it out to him.

"The old besom has the evil eye," he mutters. Then he spits. Father had told him not to spit, so he only does it when Father is not present.

Later

I was just putting my diary away and snuggling down with Snortle when Mother came up to tuck me in. I wanted to keep her, so I asked her something I had wondered about.

"Why is Cousin Anna so different from Aunt Lib? They are not one bit alike. Great-Aunt Lib is bossy and mean. Cousin Anna complains in a whine. She never finishes her sentences. Just lets them peter out."

Mother sank down on the edge of my bed but she did not answer my question.

"Mother?" I prompted.

"I'll tell you more about them one day," she said then. "Right now I need to go to bed myself. Sweet dreams, Victoria Josephine Cope."

She had trouble standing up after sitting on my low bed. She has gained weight, I think. She blew me a quick kiss and went across the hall and through the door leading into the front of the house. I could hear her starting down the stairs. She used to run down, before she started being so tired.

I wonder what she DIDN'T tell me.

In a minute I will say my prayers. I don't kneel down when Mother is not watching. God hears me just as well. I save kneeling for desperate pleas.

Snortle just pounced out from under the comforter and licked my nose. Before he will settle down, I will have to shut my eyes and pretend I am fast asleep. Then he will sigh, give up plotting to play, and go to sleep himself. He is adorable.

Saturday morning, May 29

Today the Home Girl comes. Father had a letter.

When I went down to breakfast, there he was reading last night's paper. All at once he gave a shout of laughter.

"What on earth!" Mother said, putting her hand to her heart.

"Listen to this," he said. "Your old auntie doesn't miss a trick."

Then he read out:

Mrs. Hubert Fair and her daughter Anna will be spending the next few weeks at the home of her niece, Mrs. Alastair Cope. Dr. Cope is a well-known physician in Guelph. Rev. Hubert Fair served the Knox Presbyterian Church in Hamilton for fifteen years before his death.

Mother laughed till she got a stitch in her side. She hardly ever laughs like that.

I wasn't laughing. They plan to stay a few WEEKS! What will the Home Girl be like?

Still Saturday, Bedtime

So much happened today that I can never get it all written down at one go. My hand would drop off. But I'll start.

We went and got our Home Girl. She is very small and shy. Her name is Mary Anna Wilson and she is twelve years old. She is smaller than I am and very thin. She looks as though she's ten. She won't make fun of my looks.

But let me tell it like a story even if it does have to be true. If I read it in a book, I would be fascinated.

First of all, we were late setting out. A patient arrived needing a bottle of medicine. She would stand and talk and talk. Then we no sooner got going than Bess cast a shoe and we had to stop at the smithy. I couldn't go in and watch because I was in my good dress. Peggy used to go in when we were on walks and she always came out laughing and red in the face. Her sweetheart, Joseph — well, her husband now, I suppose — is the smith's apprentice.

When we got to the station at last, there were just four children on the platform. Only one of them was a girl. She was no bigger than me. A lady was sitting on a bench next to her. All four wore labels with their names written on them, and each of them had a trunk with his or her name on it. They were big, wooden ones with brass corners. They had nothing else, just one trunk and the clothes they wore on their backs.

The lady was the only one without luggage so I was not sure she was really with them. Father must have had the same thought.

"I am Dr. Alastair Cope," he said, still sitting in the gig. "I was told to meet this train. Are you escorting these children, madam?"

The lady stood up and gave my father an annoyed glance. "We arrived almost an hour ago," she said frostily. "The train was early, admittedly, but let that pass. The two other girls I was escorting have already gone."

She reached into her large handbag and drew out some papers.

"Yes . . . Dr. Cope. I have your letter here. You reside at 264 Woolwich Street and you requested a girl to assist your wife with the housework." I could not understand why she was telling Father what he himself had written, but she went right on without giving him a chance to reply. "I have a Barnardo girl for you. The boys just happened to be on the same train. Boys are usually not escorted to their destinations. However, I have been keeping an eye on them as well as the girls."

"I am sorry to have been unavoidably delayed," Father said, his voice cool but polite. "Hold the reins, Victoria."

He got down from the Family Conveyance and reached out his hand to the lady. I gripped the reins, glad Bess was a calm horse. I could tell Father was displeased about something. He seemed to be studying the one girl waiting there. She had not looked at us or spoken a word.

"We need someone strong to help my wife," he told the woman. "That girl is nothing but a child. A sickly youngster wouldn't be worth her keep."

He did not lower his voice. The girl could not help but hear every word he spoke. I told myself she was only a Home Girl and they must be used to such things, but it was embarrassing for me. Father did not sound like himself. I knew, if I were her, each word would feel like the cut of a switch. She did not flinch, though, but stood still as stone.

"I can assure you, sir, that she is perfectly stout. We don't place girls who are not well. You are fit as a fiddle, aren't you, Mary Anna? Dr. Barnardo insists they be sound in mind and body."

I've heard Grandpa Cope describe a horse as "sound in wind and limb." The lady spoke about this Mary Anna in the very same tone of voice.

The girl had her head ducked down so far we could just see the top of her hat. She mumbled something without raising her head.

"Look at me when you speak, child," Father said, again in a sharp voice. He doesn't like children to hang their heads down as though they are ashamed of themselves. Even so, he hardly ever speaks to me that way. "What's your name?"

She stuck her chin up then. She did not look shy after all. Her eyes seemed to flash with scorn for a moment as she looked from the humiliating label to his face. Then the scorn was gone. Still, she did not smile or look at all friendly.

"My name is Mary Anna Wilson. I am strong and healthy," she said in a clear but dead voice. It sounded as though every word had been ironed flat. "I am twelve years of age."

I will not have to worry about her poking fun at me. She has pock marks on her face and her eyes are bottle green. What hair I could see was dark brown and as poker straight as mine. My hair is long enough for me to sit on if I bend my head back, but hers had been chopped off just below her ears. My nose is longer than hers but not much. Both of them tip up a bit.

"Are you a hard worker, Mary Anna?" Father asked her.

"Yes, sir," she said.

"If she does not suit your wife, write to us and we will move her," the woman said. "The smaller girls are tough and wiry, you know. They often work out better than the bigger ones. Would you like a boy?"

"No, thank you, madam," Father said, smiling at last. "I have two boys. Two great lads are all our house can hold. But one of your young fellows can hold the horse's head while I get a few more particulars and give you whatever information you wish. Jump in behind Victoria, Mary. I will only be a minute."

A little boy with red hair poking out from under his cap was standing close to Mary Anna. The lady told him to take the bridle. He ran to Bess's head.

I kept hold of the reins. I suppose Father thought Bess might be upset by his walking away while a stranger was climbing into the carriage.

The minute the girl was up the step, she tore off the label and let it drop on the station platform. Before I could see it properly, a breeze swept it away.

As Father and the lady went into the waiting room for a moment, the boy pushed his cap back and gazed up at Mary Anna. His bright hair hung in his eyes. The eyes themselves were enormous and bluer than blue. Tom's eyes are blue, but not like that. The boy's placard was turned back to front so just the blank side showed.

I cannot write another word or my hand will drop off. Also, Mother called up to blow out my candle. More tomorrow, dear Diary. I know I am breaking off just when things are getting exciting, but you'll just have to wait.

Sunday, May 30,
Morning, before anyone is up

There are so many pleasant things you are not allowed to do on the Sabbath, but writing in your diary is not one of them, thank fortune.

I'll start in where I left off. The red-haired boy spoke to our Home Girl.

"You promised Ma you'd take care of me. Now I've found you again, why can't I come with you?" he asked.

He was speaking in a low voice, afraid of being caught, but every word was clear to me. The only word I missed was a name he called her by — a nickname, I suppose. I turned to look at the girl's face. It looked frozen stiff and her eyes were like hard, green stones. She stared over his head.

"Is that your brother?" I asked.

She did not reply. She did not even glance my way.

"Jasper, don't," she said. "You know I can't do anything. As soon as I'm old enough, we'll be together as

I promised. You heard Dr. Cope say he does not need a boy."

"Will we find Emily Rose too?" he asked in a soft hopeless voice, rubbing a hole in the dirt with his boot toe.

I heard her catch her breath, but before she could speak, Father was back. He had not been away as long as it would take to buy a sack of flour. He loaded the trunk, took the reins from the boy and tossed him a penny. Then, as he climbed onto the seat, three other wagons pulled up into the space beside the railway station.

I stared at a tall boy in the first one. He sat next to two people who must have been his parents. He had such curls. They were in a big golden mop around his face. He grinned at me. I hoped they would take Jasper.

Father shook the reins and Bess began to trot.

"Goodbye, Sparrow," the boy called.

I think he said "Sparrow," although I am not sure, what with the noise of all the carriage wheels. He sounded so lonely he made me feel like bursting into tears. The girl did not answer him.

As we pulled out of the station yard, I saw that the person in the second gig was a woman who looked like a scared rabbit. Maybe she thought the children were criminals the way Mother had said. If she did, she was wrong. They looked fine, just tired. I smiled at her but she did not smile back. I didn't notice who was in the other wagon.

Father said not a word to either of us. He looked as though something had made him angry. I glanced back as Bess began to trot along, keeping pace with the rest of the traffic crowding the street. The girl's green eyes were no longer like stone. They were filled with tears. She did not catch my look, I think, for I turned at once to face front again. I could feel my cheeks burn as though I had been spying.

Since it was market day, the streets were crowded with people and animals. All the dogs in Guelph seemed to be ducking in and out among the carriage wheels. Men were insulting each other's driving and their wives were calling out greetings to each other. The horses neighed back and forth, as though they too had friends there. Maybe all the noise was why Father stayed so silent. I wished he would speak to the Home Girl so she would feel welcome, but I could not think what to say myself.

I sat there and tried to imagine feeling really sad about being parted from David or Tom. I don't think I'd shed a tear for David. I am fond of Tom. I can't imagine weeping over him though.

I'll leave the shock we had when we got home until later. It was catastrophic.

Afternoon

Here comes the shock, Diary!
When we got home yesterday, a hackney from the

station was in front of our house. The driver was muttering things as he carried a trunk in on his shoulder. Great-Aunt Lib and Cousin Anna had come a day early and, even though I tried hard to feel welcoming toward them, I took one look at their sour faces and felt sorry for myself instead.

I forgot it was Saturday in all the bustle of new people, but trust Mother not to forget our Saturday night baths. It is a big job seeing to it that the entire family is clean for Sunday. In Mother's mind, cleanliness isn't NEXT to godliness; they are equals, part and parcel of the same thing. This time, she got David to bring in extra buckets of water to heat while she was off settling Aunt Lib and Cousin Anna in the spare room they are going to share.

Then she collared Mary Anna and me and marched us down to the kitchen for our Saturday night bath. We both felt shy, even though there was a screen to hide behind. Since I was to go first, I turned my back to her and took off my clothes and climbed into the big tin tub. I started washing myself while Mother chatted with Mary Anna.

"Would you mind if we just called you Mary?" she asked our Home Girl. "I'm afraid we might get two Annas confused."

"No, ma'am," the Home Girl said. But her voice sounded funny.

I would not want to be called Josephine because another Victoria was around the house. I am Victoria.

I decided, then and there, to call her Mary Anna, whatever the rest did.

Then I heard Mary Anna say, "Ma'am, they hunted through our heads when we left England, when we got to Hazelbrae and again the night before we left. If there's a nit left in my hair, he's a brave beast."

She was being polite but she still sounded fed up.

She has an accent. It isn't cockney but it is very British. I cannot write down how it sounds, just what it says. I don't like books where they talk Scots or something and you can't just read along because you keep having to translate the words.

I could have told her Mother would check her head anyway. She won't have a louse in the house.

Then I climbed out and dried myself fast and pulled on my nightgown. While Mother did my hair up in rags, which are lumpy and only give me curls for half the morning, Mary Anna was scrubbing herself from head to toe. Mother let her use the lavender soap she makes. I could tell Mary Anna was not used to soap that smelled so sweet, but she did not say so. She just put it up to her nose, took a deep breath and smiled. I think that was her first smile in our house.

So the two of us were ready for church this morning.

Father is planning to have a bathroom built in our house with hot water that comes into the bathtub from a tap. They have one at my friend Eliza Miller's house, but her father is a judge. They moved away a month ago and I miss her and her sister sorely. When Tom and I went to Sunday School, our class was so different with her gone. I do like Roberta Johns though. I've never noticed her much because I was Eliza's friend, but Roberta could be a good friend too. I wonder if she likes me.

I saw Moses following Mary Anna to her bed in Peggy's old room. No rubber sheet for her. She looked down at our cat and smiled in a way that tells me she might be my friend, if she wasn't a Home Girl. It is hard to know how to act to a girl who is smaller than I am and only one year older.

Evening

The Sabbath is supposed to be a day of rest, but it is one of the busiest days we have. There's a saying that goes, "No rest for the wicked." On Sunday it should say, "No rest for the godly." The wicked can loll around all day, if they choose. We good Presbyterians have no time for lolling. First of all, we go to church three times and we have to wear our Sunday clothes from morning to night and keep them clean. We are supposed to think holy thoughts too. I am glad they can't check up on what is inside our heads. We have to have some scripture verses off by memory every week, and every week we forget until the last minute. This week I had to learn the 23rd Psalm, and that was lucky since I already knew it. Tom had trouble with his piece and Father made him do it over and over because he kept putting in wrong words.

When I came down to breakfast, Mary Anna was already hard at work. I thought about saying, "Good morning," but her face was like a closed door with a sign saying: PRIVATE. NO TRESPASSING. It looked as though she'd starched it until it was stiff. I wonder if she had to keep it clenched that way so she would not cry. Her eyes stayed cast down and did not meet anyone else's.

I took my bowl of porridge from Mother and sat down. Mary Anna must have eaten hers earlier. She never stopped working.

Then David arrived. He plunked himself down and ordered Mary Anna to fetch him his porridge. He spoke to her roughly, as though she were his slave. He spoke extra loudly, too, as if she were deaf.

"David Cope, mind your manners," Mother said. She was busy getting something for Father and missed seeing him glower.

When Mary Anna set his porridge bowl down in front of him, he dug his spoon in without saying thank you. Sometimes he makes me ashamed. I heard Father say once that his brain is coldly analytical. I think his heart is too.

"Now we are all here, let us ask God's blessing on our food," Father said.

David had to drop his spoon fast. At least we don't have to kneel. When Mother was a child, they all knelt while their father prayed, and by the time he said Amen, the food was stone cold. My father knows better. He always says short blessings.

We are supposed to love the Sabbath Day and keep it holy. That means we can't play games and we have to read books that are good for us, like *Pilgrim's Progress* or *The Wide, Wide World.* Mother chooses. Sometimes we enjoy them. We just finished *Uncle Tom's Cabin*, which was very good, I must admit.

Thinking of the slave auction in it reminded me of Father and my going to the station and getting Mary Anna. I told Father so when we went for our Sunday walk together. He laughed.

"No, Vic," he said. "You had to pay for slaves. Home Children are free. The Home actually pays something toward their keep at first."

He sounded angry again. I could not think why. It must be something he has found out about which is unfit for children to hear. Mother has a long list of such things. I do my level best to find out all about them without letting anyone know.

That's how I discovered what's happened to Peggy. Our neighbour, Mrs. Cameron, told Mother that not only is Peggy married now, but she's going to have a baby. I cannot imagine Peggy being anyone's mother. I would love to ask Mother questions about this, but I know she would not tell me a thing.

I got this much by overhearing the two of them talking. Mrs. Cameron knows all the gossip and spills it into Mother's ears. "Just one juicy morsel after another," Father says.

Mother works on her mending or embroiders whenever Mrs. C. is speaking, but she does not miss one word. Every so often she exclaims, "Oh, no, Mrs. Cameron. I'm sure you are mistaken."

Then Mrs. Cameron goes on to prove she is right by giving more gory details. She says Mrs. Dougal, who is coming to help with the heavy work, is "a bit mum but a good worker."

Mrs. Cameron is NOT mum at all. Last time she came, she said a dog was "bisected" by a wagon wheel on the main street of Guelph. I asked Mother what "bisected" meant exactly, and got scolded for eaves-dropping. I still don't know. Father would tell me to look it up in *Webster's Dictionary*. Maybe I will.

We sang my favourite hymn in church. "Fight the Good Fight." Mary Anna came to church with us, but she did not sing. I wonder why. I could tell she knew the hymns. I saw her lips move while we sang "Stand Up, Stand Up for Jesus."

During the evening service, Father fell asleep and began to snore softly.

"Poke him, Victoria," Mother whispered. She was blushing with humiliation.

I dug my elbow into his waistcoat and he woke up with a start and hollered out, "What's the matter, Lily?" Then he took in where he was and bowed his head fast as though he were praying for forgiveness. I was sitting next to him, though. He was laughing! I could feel a huge laugh about to burst out of me until I looked at Mother. I don't know how she does it, but she can stop a laugh with one sad look.

Time to sleep now.

My new room,
Late afternoon, Monday, May 31

Cousin Anna and Aunt Lib were supposed to share the spare room, but this morning Cousin A. went on and on about being such a light sleeper and how she needs her rest because she is delicate. (She should try sleeping with a pug puppy.) So I had to move in with Mary Anna. Tom cleared out of the boys' room into mine, which is too small for a visitor. Cousin A. gets the big front room the boys had. David will sleep on the sofa in the parlour. It's like a game of Musical Bedrooms. It won't bother David much. When school lets out, he's going to Grandpa Cope's farm. He's going to get paid and work as a hired man.

So poor Mary Anna cannot have a room to herself until Aunt Lib and Cousin Anna leave us. She will sleep on the old truckle bed and I will have the cot she was using. I'm sitting on it now, stealing a little time to write before I have to help with supper.

Mother said that this was a small room for two, but it wouldn't be for long. (She must be forgetting that other time when their visit lasted nearly six weeks!)

Six weeks squeezed into Peggy's little bedroom is like being exiled, but I am very interested in Mary Anna and I'll get to know her much better now we are sharing a room.

I can just imagine what Nellie Bigelow would say if she had to sleep in the same room as a Home Child. She would expire on the spot. She is sure to be mean as dirt to Mary Anna. She called me a snob today because I made a face when she blew her nose like a trumpet. Mother went to school with Nellie's mother and she says Nellie sounds just like her. "Just remember, Victoria, how lucky you are to have me for your mother instead of Bertha Bigelow," she said once. She is right.

There's a serial in the newspaper called "The Orphan Girl" or "The Darker Side of Life." Nellie should read it.

Mother sent Mary Anna and me up to change the beds before I left for school this morning. Snortle had wakened me early and so there was still time. We didn't say much but I liked doing it together. It was almost like having a sister.

David would be shocked at that idea. To him, a Home Girl is a servant, not a friend and never a sister! Sometimes I am almost sorry for David. He cuts himself off from people. In Geography I learned that an island is a body of land entirely surrounded by water. Well, David is an island of David entirely surrounded by David.

I know that sounds daft, dear Diary, but I know what I mean.

I brought my hairbrush and comb and nightgown down the hall to our room before I left too. Snortle followed me as usual and stared around at everything.

"I hope you won't mind Snortle being with us," I said to Mary Anna, who was rearranging things in the chest of drawers. I don't know what I'd have done if she had answered that she could not sleep in the same room with a dog. But she didn't.

"Who could mind Snortle?" she said with a flicker of a smile.

Her smiles are gone so fast they are like hummingbirds.

"Take care of him tomorrow while I'm at school," I said.

She nodded. It will be nice for him to have her, but I felt a twinge of jealousy. I wish he was like Mary's little lamb and could follow me to school each day. Tomorrow Mary Anna is going to be starting school, so he'll have to follow Mother around. He is not fond of Aunt Lib or Cousin Anna.

There is no rubber sheet on this bed. Mother did not mention it and I am pretending I forgot.

Later, After ten

When we had blown out the candle and were waiting to go to sleep, I took a deep breath and asked

Mary Anna about that little boy, Jasper. I've been longing to ever since we came home from the station that first day.

"Is he your brother? Did he come with you? That lady said the boys came from somewhere else."

She did not answer.

"Are you asleep, Mary Anna?" I said.

She pretended she was. I listened to her breathing. She wasn't. But I let her go on play-acting. I'll ask again when I know her better.

It is nice that I can relight my candle without waking her —

As I wrote those words, the door opened a crack and Moses pushed her way in. She ignored me but went and jumped up next to Mary Anna. I think I saw Mary Anna shift a little to make room, but maybe I imagined it.

June

Tuesday, June 1, After breakfast

We have to leave for school soon but I just have to write about what happened at breakfast. Mother called Mary Anna at half-past five. Yesterday she let her sleep until seven since she was not going to school until she had had a day to settle in. Now she has to go down and get the stove lighted, bring in water and put some on to heat for washing and tea, set the table and start the breakfast.

Once Mary Anna had tiptoed away, though, Snortle saw no reason not to start the day, and tried to tug off my blankets. I gave in and got up too. I felt strange about Mary Anna having to get up so much earlier than me. It is funny because I never once felt guilty about Peggy getting up so early, and I could always hear her banging about. Mary Anna is nearer my age, of course, and sharing a room makes me feel different about her. Anyway, I got washed and dressed fast and was down a lot earlier than usual.

Aunt Lib was already seated at the kitchen table. Maybe she never went to bed. She sat up stiff as a poker and glared at each person as he or she arrived, as though anybody not down and dressed by sunrise was a sluggard and a backslider.

I stared at her, and for the first time I saw how very old she looks. Her skin looks like the old leather gloves Mother uses for gardening. She has dark spots all over her hands, and WHISKERS! She caught me staring.

"Well, Miss, you'll know me next time we meet," she snapped.

She sounded so cranky that Snortle growled at her.

"Sorry, Auntie," I said. But I nearly laughed.

Before I sat at the table Mother unplaited my braids and brushed them out without saying anything. I can do it myself, but she does a far better job.

After school

I'll start right in because I had more to tell when we had to leave.

Aunt Lib caught sight of Mary Anna. She stared at her the way you might look at a slug. Then she said, "That girl is scrawny as a picked chicken. How the doctor thinks she will be any real help with the work, I fail to see."

She always talks about Father like that, calling him "the doctor." Nobody knew what to say. She goes on and on about our bad manners, but she is far ruder. She saw we were shocked because her cheeks reddened a bit. But she was not ashamed of herself. She thinks whatever she does is right.

"And why, pray tell, is she wearing a good dress to do housework?" she demanded.

"Mary Anna is dressed for school," Mother said quietly. "I helped her choose what dress to wear last evening."

I was there when Mother went through Mary Anna's Barnardo trunk. The clothes were made to measure before she left England. But she must have grown taller and thinner during the voyage and at Hazelbrae. She said she was terribly seasick. But a couple of the dresses still fitted, and Mother said another two can be altered. None of them is really pretty, though. There are no ruffles or braid trim or nice buttons. There are boots and underclothes and a tam and a shawl. She only has one good dress to wear to church, and Mother told her she was going to have to wear the church one to school too, on the first day at least, until she and Mrs. Dougal can get to work and fix up some of the others.

Mary Anna offered to stay home, but Mother was having none of that. I could have told Mary Anna to save her breath to cool her porridge. My parents are bound and bent on getting us all the best education possible. And that includes Home Girls.

"School!" Aunt Lib squawked, straightening up as though someone had put a pistol to her head. Her eyes popped so wide open they looked as though they might fall out. "Surely she won't be going to school."

Mother told her that Mary Anna was going to school with me this morning. She spoke in such a cool voice I thought Aunt Lib would drop the subject. She didn't.

"What use will she have for book learning? You can teach her to be a good housewife right here. Anna never went to school."

"I know," Mother said.

I can't explain how she said those two words. But it seemed as though she'd said much more. After a funny little pause, she went on, "Mary is only twelve. She will be company for Victoria when Thomas goes to the collegiate in September."

"Thank heavens she's not going to the collegiate," David muttered.

Mother just looked at him, one of those looks that makes you feel less than an inch tall.

"Excuse me," he said, and bolted.

"It's nonsensical," Aunt Lib said, as though David did not exist. "I thought this Home Girl was to be a help, not just an extra mouth to feed."

Mother looked at the breakfast on Aunt Lib's plate, but did not answer back or try to argue with her. I was glad. Aunt Lib never changes her mind about anything no matter how long you try to set her straight. But Aunt Lib still did not give up. She said she had heard Home Children were mostly workhouse brats who would do well to learn to write their names.

"Your cousin Albert says they are all mentally defective. And many are diseased," she said.

Mother had sent Mary Anna out for more water, but she returned just in time to catch these last words. She set the pail down with a clang and went to poke the fire. Her face looked hotter than the stove.

"Aunt Lib, that is more than enough. The child has ears and she is a stranger in our midst," Mother snapped. "I will not have you speaking about her as though she is a stick of wood."

Aunt Lib tossed her head and gave a snort. Cousin Anna gave a gasp of fright. Mother glanced at her and spoke more gently, all about their agreeing to send Mary Anna to school, and it was not as though they had farm chores for her to do. Then she told them Father had hired Mrs. Dougal.

"You know," she ended up, "Mary Anna can read and reckon as well as most Canadian children her age."

Father came in then and asked Cousin Anna if she had slept any more soundly. Mother ordered Mary Anna and me up to strip the beds, since we were early still. I did mine like lightning so I could write down the horrible scene at breakfast before I forgot. I have never been ashamed of one of my grown-up relatives before, but listening to Aunt Lib being so heartless made me feel sick at my stomach. Now I must RUN!

After supper

Mother thinks I am studying, but I have more to tell.

The three of us left for school together. Tom often goes with one of his friends, but today he came along as if he thought we needed his support. Maybe we did. We met Mrs. Dougal coming up our walk. She bobbed her head slightly and went on in without a word.

I thought Mary Anna might chat with us as we went, but she just plodded down the road two paces behind. When I told her to come on, she looked at the ground and kept trudging step by step without speeding up one bit. Finally I stopped trying to jolly her along. Truth to tell, I almost forgot she was back there. We arrived just as the last bell finished ringing. Everyone had gone inside.

When we walked in, the whole class stared at our Home Girl. The older girls looked her up and down as though she were some rare specimen on display at the fall fair. A two-headed calf maybe.

"Oh, it's just their Home Girl," Polly Sampson said to Nellie. "My mother was talking to Mrs. Cope at church and she said they were getting one. I didn't think she'd come to school with us, though."

Mary Anna and I both looked away and pretended we had not heard. It was cowardly of me, maybe, but I couldn't help it. I did not know what to say. I needed words to crush her and I could not think of any.

Mr. Grigson took one glance and sent Mary Anna to sit at the back of the classroom in the row he saves for idiots and foreigners and the foundling boy who was left on the steps of the county home when he was a baby.

Two years ago Mrs. Symes, the Baptist minister's widow, took him to live with her here in Guelph. She told my mother he was "right handy" and she really likes him. His name is Jed Pryor and he's smart, even though he never says a word. I saw him reading *A Tale of Two Cities* once. He'd taken it from the shelf at the back of the room. He hid it in his desk until he finished it, and Mr. Grigson never missed it.

I did not object to where Mr. Grigson put Mary Anna. It wouldn't have done her any good if I had. Maybe she'll feel more at home back there and she'll be safer. He mostly ignores the back-row pupils. He only notices them when he's furious for no good reason and wants somebody to roar at. Nobody will complain to the school trustees about his treatment of those children.

It turns out Mother was quite right about Mary Anna's learning. She can figure as well as I can. She can read too, but not as well as I. She gets the words right but they come out slowly, without what Mother calls "expression." Mother and Father have read aloud to us ever since we were babies. I suppose nobody has listened to Mary Anna reading. Hearing her is like watching someone walking across a sheet of ice. You keep wanting to put your hand out to steady her in case she falls. But you don't and she doesn't.

"Well, that is proficient," Mr. Grigson said after Mary Anna had read a few passages. He sounded surprised and somehow insulting. I got a funny feeling he was disappointed.

Then Nellie Bigelow demanded that Mary Anna move over a few seats. She had been right behind Nellie's desk.

"Everybody knows those Home Kids have nits," she said, tossing her mane of hair around as if she were a horse. She has a long face and her laugh is a definite whinny. It's strange how nice a horse looks and how unpleasant the same features are on Nellie.

I almost told her right out that Mary Anna is free from bugs because Mother checked. Then I saw Mary Anna's eyes looking right at me and I knew she was praying I would not say a word. So I didn't.

We went home at noon, as usual. I talked a lot, as usual. Mary Anna might have told about her morning, but she eats in the kitchen. I am sure she would not have said a word about school anyway. Absolutely, positively, sure.

As soon as we got back to school Tom ran to join the bigger boys. Mary Anna and I went over to where the girls were gathered under some trees in the corner of the schoolyard. She hung back though. She sat herself down in a fence corner where there was no shade. I suppose I should have called to her to join the rest of us, but I couldn't. She had made her choice. If she had sat down next to me, I would not have moved away. I don't think she likes us.

I do not agree with David about Home Children, but I guess they really are different from us. If they weren't, they would not have left their families in England. If something happened to my father and we had no money, we would go straight to Uncle Peter or our grandparents. Everybody has relatives.

She took out a book and kept her head bent over it. Yet she never once turned a page. I watched out of the corner of my eye. We played red rover and tag and started on a game of hopscotch. I tried to enjoy myself, but I was glad when the teacher rang the bell.

I looked at Mary Anna's book later. It was *Elsie Dinsmore*. No wonder she did not keep turning pages. Elsie is such a namby-pamby prig that nobody could keep caring about her. Even Beth March in *Little Women*, who is a bit too good, is one hundred times more alive than Elsie.

When we came home after four, Aunt Lib and Cousin Anna were in the kitchen. I burst in with things to tell but the looks on their faces shut me up.

"Girl, fetch me a fresh cup of tea," Aunt Lib rapped out before Mary Anna had put down her books.

"All right, Auntie," I sang out, moving to the stove fast.

Aunt Lib reached out with her cane and caught my leg.

"Not you, Missy, and well you know it," she barked.

Mary Anna was filling her cup without a word when I got away and came up here to write.

Later

The minute I got downstairs again, Cousin Anna said she was so sorry, but she had broken a tiny ornament in my room. It was my little statue of a shepherdess, which my old Sunday School teacher had given me as a keepsake before she got married and moved to Waterloo. I have had my shepherdess since I was seven. I loved her. I even named her Lucette. I could not say a word. I just turned my back and tried not to let her see I was crying.

"I'm truly sorry, Victoria dear," she said in a voice like treacle. "My scarf caught it and swept it off the dresser. It was only a cheap little thing or it wouldn't have overbalanced so easily. You should put things well back from the edge, dear, if you want to keep them safe."

Lucette sat safely on my chest of drawers for over four years without once overbalancing. I hate Cousin Anna. What was she doing in my room anyway? She's ugly. I could not say, "Don't worry. It's all right." It was NOT all right.

Why does she let herself look so awful? She wears spectacles which are scratched and always dirty and she wears shoes which clunk like horses' hooves. Her clothes are either grey or black and they look drab. Her hair is pulled back into a tight knob. She smiles all the time, but none of the smiles are real or happy. Her eyes dart around, watching for you to do something she can tattle to Mother. I wish Snortle would bite her.

I don't believe she was ever a child. I think she was born a schemer and a whiner.

It is funny how writing it all down in black and white makes me feel better. It's like when Mother lanced the boil on Tom's neck last summer and pus poured out. He said it felt way better the minute she let out the poison.

While I was picking the bits of Lucette out of my wastepaper basket, Mrs. Dougal, who was still tidying up, came by with a mop in her hand. She stopped, looked at Lucette, clicked her tongue in what seemed a sympathetic way, and walked on down the hall. Not one word did she utter. I wrapped the bits of china carefully in a soft handkerchief Grandma Sinclair gave me. It has tiny daisies embroidered in the corner. Then Mrs. Dougal brought me an empty candy box which still smells of chocolates. It was just the right size to hold the pieces.

Before I could thank her properly she was gone again, never saying a word. I like her a lot.

I put Lucette's broken body in my treasure box, which is a cedar chest Father gave me when I turned nine. I will keep her forever. I do not think I can ever forgive C.A.

Evening, About eight o'clock

After supper, Mother suddenly announced that she wanted Thomas to help Mary Anna with the dishes because she had a job for me to do upstairs. When we got to her room, she sat down and pushed her little footstool over to me.

"Sit down, Victoria. I can feel you are bursting with some tale of outrage, and it is time to get it off your chest."

I don't know how she always knows, but I poured out the whole story. Then, "Why *is* Cousin Anna so different from Aunt Lib?" I asked her again. "Great-Aunt Lib is so bossy and Cousin Anna is always so whiny. She says she doesn't mean to fuss, and then she goes ahead and fusses. I think they are both awful."

Mother stroked my head and was quiet.

"Why don't they look alike?" I asked her. "They don't, you know. You'd never guess they were related."

Mother smiled, and then astonished me by saying, "It is time you were told some family history. They don't look related because they aren't."

I was leaning against her but I jerked up straight and stared.

"What?" I gasped. "They must be!"

Diary, you will not believe what she told me. Cousin Anna isn't Aunt Lib's daughter! Not only that, but they aren't even blood relatives. Aunt Lib's husband, Hubert Fair, was a Presbyterian minister. Mother was afraid of him when she was small. He never laughed, and she thought his smile was cold. He had a twin brother, Humphrey, who married a woman with a little girl named Anna.

When Mother said "a little girl named Anna" it began to sound like a fairy tale. I wasn't even surprised when the child's parents died in a typhoid epidemic and she was left an orphan.

Aunt Lib's husband went to the funeral in Winnipeg without her. He told the lawyers, without saying a word to Aunt Lib, that they wanted to adopt his brother's step-daughter. Then he brought the three-year-old home with him. Aunt Lib, who had never gotten along well with children, was handed a spoiled and lonely little girl. "This is your new daughter," her husband announced.

"She must have been so happy to have a baby at last," I said. I felt thrilled at the way it was turning out.

Mother's smile looked twisted and her voice grew sharp.

"No, Victoria. Anna was not a sweet little baby. She was almost four and she was wished on Aunt Lib without either of them having any say in the matter. Don't forget that Uncle Hubert was only her step-uncle. She barely knew him. And he commanded her to call them Father and Mother."

"She must have been angry . . . confused too," I said slowly. I couldn't think of one word to express all she must have felt. Frightened. Forsaken. So lonely.

Mother nodded her head. "Whenever she annoys me, I try to think of what the two of them had to deal with. Aunt Lib thought Anna was badly brought up, and set out to change things overnight. Poor little Anna might have turned to her uncle, but he was a busy man who believed raising children was women's work. Anna was old enough to know that nobody really wanted her."

"Oh, poor Cousin Anna," I whispered.

"Indeed. Then, when she was twelve, Uncle Hubert died. He left instructions in his will that Anna was to be raised as his daughter. So the two of them were trapped, with no way out."

I asked why Cousin Anna didn't leave when she grew up.

Mother said she couldn't. Cousin Anna was supposed to be delicate, too, so she was educated at home.

"Who taught her?" I wanted to know.

Mother said Uncle Hubert taught her to read and do arithmetic. He thought any learning beyond that was wasted on a girl. Aunt Lib taught her what a housewife should know — how to make bread, how to darn a sock, how to play hymns on the parlour organ. "They assumed she would marry, of course. She didn't. The only place she could have met a young man was at church, with her mother's eagle eye watching her every move. She has no money of her own. She earns her keep by running errands, preparing meals, listening to Aunt Lib complain, doing things for the church."

"I'd run away," I said.

"Running away takes courage, Victoria. You need food and shelter. . . . Never mind. Time you went to bed."

I got up and then just stood there. I was struggling to believe what Mother had said. Aunt Lib was NOT Cousin Anna's mother, and, what's more, Cousin Anna was not really related to me.

"Jumping Jehosaphat!" I whispered.

"Victoria Josephine Cope, please do not use such vulgar expressions," Mother said sternly, but with a smile in her eyes.

She had trouble standing up after sitting so long. I helped pull her upright.

"Remember that the story I just told you is our secret," she said as I started for the door. "I thought it might help you to survive the weeks ahead."

So, dear Diary, what do you think of all that?

Nearly ten, In bed

Snortle just tried his usual trick — pouncing out from under the comforter to lick my nose. Pesky Snortle. I make enough ink blots myself, without his wiggling and pouncing. But once I close my eyes and he thinks I'm fast asleep he will usually settle down too.

I wish I could tell Mary Anna and Tom about Aunt Lib and Anna. I wish Mother had not made me promise.

Very late

I was almost asleep when Mary Anna began talking. She had gone to sleep long before. Most of it was just muttering, but she finally called out names. Things like, "I'm coming, Jasper," or, "Where are you? Emily Rose is so heavy. I'm coming."

She sounded so upset that I got out of bed and shook her shoulder. When she gasped and her eyes flew wide open, I could tell she did not recognize me. She looked terrified. I told her she had been dreaming. Then I asked again who Jasper was. I meant to be tactful but the question burst out.

Mary Anna turned to stone at my words. She did not answer either, just rolled over and faced the wall.

When I was sure she was asleep, I thought of you, Diary. Snortle snortled with disgust at being disturbed, but I ignored him. I needed to put my sadness down. Yet now I have written it out, I am still sad.

And VERY sleepy.

Wednesday, June 2, Bedtime

Tonight nothing seems worth writing.

We had liver and prunes for supper. And I bit my tongue. It is still very sore. Did Louisa May Alcott have days like this? Did they make her a better writer?

I thought Aunt Lib and Cousin A. might be nicer now I know about their past. They were not. Aunt Lib made me go back and wash my hands when they were perfectly clean. Anna gave a shiver when I laughed. As if I had hurt her delicate ears!

I am hoping for a pleasanter tomorrow.

Thursday, June 3

I really like Roberta Johns. She has been in my class all year, but I'm just getting to know her now. You will see what I mean, Diary, when I tell you how she helped Mary Anna out this morning.

Mr. Grigson sent the two of them to the board. I could see that Mary Anna was nervous. The teacher is frightening. Tom says it is because of his eyebrows, which are bushy and dark and glower at you. But the eyes glower too and he growls.

He likes giving boys the strap. He even strapped Tom once, and Tom is polite to him and a good scholar. He does not strap us girls, but I think it is because he despises us.

Only boys matter.

Anyway, Roberta saw Mary Anna had made two mistakes and, when Mr. Grigson's back was turned, Roberta showed Mary Anna what she had done wrong. She did it so fast that I doubt anybody but me saw. When the teacher looked at what she'd written, he said, "Well, Miss, I see you are a cut above most of your kind. Most of the waifs and strays shipped over by those British Do-Gooders are subnormal at best. But this is passable work."

I longed to shout something, but what? He gets livid at what he calls "insubordination." I did open my mouth but no words came out.

Tom spoke up though. "Mary Anna is not a waif or a stray," he said in a most polite voice. "She has a good brain and better manners than many of the people in this class."

"Silence, young man. One more such remark and I'll need to get out my strap," Mr. Grigson thundered.

Tom did not say anything more. He did not need to. I was proud he was my brother. Mary Anna's face grew pink, but her eyes shone when she looked at Tom.

When we came out for afternoon recess, I looked for Roberta and asked if she'd like to skip. Mary Anna would not join in, but I saw her lips moving as we chanted the rhymes. When we stopped turning the rope, I pulled Mary Anna over to where Roberta was standing and asked Roberta if she'd like to walk home with us. Tom goes with the older boys on the way home.

"I would," Roberta said, "but I can't stay out and play. My little sister Hannah is just three and she's been sick. Mother has so much work to do that I try to mind Hannah for her. Even though she is not strong, she's an imp. Yesterday she somehow tipped Mother's container of starch into the laundry tub and all of Dad's handkerchiefs came out stiff as boards. He'll never be able to blow his nose on them. You can see why she needs watching."

"She sounds like a — " I started and then stopped.

"I know she does," Roberta laughed, "but we thought we were going to lose her last winter when she got pneumonia. It was dreadful. It was as though the sun had stopped shining."

"I have a little sister too," Mary Anna said all of a sudden, scaring me out of my wits. "I know how you felt."

I tried not to let my excitement show.

Roberta asked what the sister's name was. Just as though Mary was not a Home Girl.

"Victoria knows," she answered, her voice hard. "Her name is Emily Rose Wilson. Jasper Jacob is my brother. Victoria saw him at the station."

I wanted to ask one hundred more questions, but I managed to hold my tongue. It was not easy. Even my beloved Grandma Sinclair once told me my tongue was attached in the middle and wagged at both ends.

I hoped Roberta would ask more and she did, but Mother is coming up the back stairs. I'm supposed to be asleep. I'll be back as soon as I can, Diary.

Friday, June 4, Early morning

I made myself wake early so I could write more. Mary Anna is not even awake. Even Snortle is still snoring. I'll have to write fast. But it is so interesting.

Yesterday Roberta asked the questions I dared not utter.

"Is your little sister in England, Mary?" she asked softly.

Mary Anna did not speak for at least a minute. Then she burst out, "No, she is not in England."

We stared at her. She sounded so fierce. Then more words poured out. "They separated the girls from the boys on the train, but I still had Emily Rose and I watched over her the best I could. When we got to Hazelbrae in Peterborough, they took her from me and put her with other babies. We had only been there two days when they gave her to a man and woman who had no children."

"Oh, Mary Anna!" Roberta cried. Her voice was filled with sorrow.

Oh, I so want to keep writing, but Mary Anna has thrown off her covers, Snortle is up and prancing, and Mother is calling.

After school

Mary Anna told us that when her mother took them to Dr. Barnardo's, she told them she did not want her children to be adopted by strangers. She was sure she could get work and come back for them. A friend of her father's had been helping them a bit.

"But the Hazelbrae people told me Mother wasn't coming back," Mary Anna said, her face stony. "They said she would want Emily Rose adopted by a couple who could give her a good home. One lady told me to forget my mother."

"As if you could!" Roberta cried.

They would not tell Mary Anna the name or address of the people who took her sister.

Just as she told us this, the bell rang for us to go back in. My head was fairly buzzing and I could not keep my mind on Grammar or Geography.

At home, Mother had lots of things saved up for Mary Anna to do. Most days, Mrs. Dougal leaves our house at five. We eat our supper in the dining room. Lucky Mary Anna, eating in the kitchen with only Snortle and Moses for company.

Oh, no! Mother is calling me already.

Ten minutes later

It was not suppertime. Mother just wanted to know if I had seen the potato masher. Why would I?

Anyway, when I came in from school, I tried my best to slide through the kitchen without getting caught, because I was longing to write in you, dear Diary. But Mother gave me a look which said I had to sit and visit with Aunt Lib and Cousin Anna. Aunt Lib never stops criticizing and Cousin Anna puts in little mean digs at me. She is hard to bear in other ways too. She waits until I'm halfway up the stairs and calls me back to shut the door.

I keep reminding myself of little orphan Anna long ago, but it does not seem real.

And now, before I write anything important, she's calling me back down to set the table for supper. Ugh!

Bedtime

We had no sooner finished supper than Roberta was knocking at our back door. She looked so excited. She dragged me outside to tell me that her uncle has taken a Home Boy. She does not know his name, so he might be Jasper!

The Johns only heard about him today. Roberta's uncle will be coming in to market tomorrow morning and he'll have the boy with him.

"I'll come over right after breakfast," she said. "Your place is on the way."

"Maybe I can talk Mother into letting Mary Anna come too," I told her. I felt like dancing. It will be so perfect if her uncle has Jasper. Roberta is as excited as I am.

I could hardly wait to tell Mary Anna the news. I ran inside, but I got caught by Cousin Anna wanting her yarn held. I tried to escape but Mother gave me her withering look again, and I couldn't.

Cousin Anna is so slow. When I hold the yarn for Mother, she talks to me, telling me stories or reciting poems she learned as a girl. Cousin Anna just sits like a lump or lectures me on being a better daughter. I feel as though moss is growing on me while I sit and sit.

Finally I was free. I raced upstairs. Mary Anna, who has a cold in the head for sure, was getting into her nightgown. Usually I would turn my back until she was dressed, but I couldn't wait. When she heard, she was as thrilled as I.

"I don't think I'll be able to get away," she said. Her eyes were huge and they shone like carriage lamps, but she did not jump up and down or shriek the way I had. She said she would have chores to do since Saturday Mrs. Dougal does not come. I told Mary Anna that my mother would give in right away when I told her the whole story.

Mary Anna put her hand out as though she was covering my mouth. "You mustn't tell her," she begged me. "They told us at the Home not to dwell upon our families and act homesick. They said we would only make trouble for ourselves if we complained."

"That Dr. Barnardo sounds terrible — " I began to say.

"No, he is NOT," Mary Anna flashed back. "He's a true gentleman. He remembers all our names and he cares about each one. It's the people who work for him . . . "

It doesn't make sense to me, but they certainly convinced Mary Anna. I think she is being silly but, in the end, I promised not to tell.

It will be hard to get to sleep tonight, knowing I might be seeing Jasper tomorrow. I'll have to get Roberta's uncle to bring him over to our house to see his sister. I won't tell her that. It'll be a better surprise and, if it doesn't come true, her heart won't be broken.

Later

Mary Anna is asleep at last. I put my diary away and tried to sleep, but I couldn't. Nobody has the right to take away a child's family. I don't see how Mary Anna's mother could have sent them all so far away. She must have been trying to help them somehow, but it is cruel to Mary Anna. I must find out more and do all I can to help her make her feel at home here.

She looks terribly tired over there on her truckle bed. I wonder how I would feel if I went to England as a Canadian Home Girl. I cannot imagine it, try as I will.

Saturday, June 5, Early morning

I'm writing in here while I wait for Roberta to come. Mother says Mary Anna cannot come to market with me. If she had not caught a bad cold, Mother might have weakened. But she says Mary Anna needs to spend the day quietly at home.

Roberta will be here any minute. I must run.

Afternoon

The boy was not Jasper. He was one of the others at the station though. He remembered Father and me coming. He and Jasper had been together at the Barnardo home in Toronto. He thought a lady took Jasper, even though she said he was too small.

But that was all he could tell us. He didn't know her name or where she came from. Roberta's uncle took him away before the lady and Jasper left.

Roberta's uncle called the boy away then. The market is so crowded and everyone is so busy. They really had no time to spare. There was one woman there with a box filled with free kittens. Mother would not take one, but it was hard to walk on by.

I was surprised to find that, worried as I was, my mouth began to water when I passed a table filled with fresh-baked bread. I felt as though I could have eaten a whole loaf. Then Roberta, who was feeling the same way, begged her uncle for some pennies and we bought two fat cinnamon buns stuck full of raisins.

They tasted like the food they eat in Heaven, whatever it is.

The first strawberries were there and they smelled delicious too. We always get lots from Grandma Cope's farm.

Diary, don't tell anyone. I stole two berries. The box was heaped high. Not even Roberta noticed. They tasted like all of summer rolled up into a mouth-watering ball. God did not mind.

But I felt anxious on the way over to Roberta's house. I couldn't help it. Her little sister Hannah came racing out to meet us, though, and cheered me up. She's funny and sweet, but so thin, and her skin is so white it is almost pale blue. Something is wrong with her heart. They can't operate on a heart, of course. Roberta does not say, but I think they are always afraid Hannah may die. She seems so frail and she grows breathless whenever she runs the least bit. I had not seen much of her because she often stays home from church. Mr. Johns and Roberta and her brother Lou come, but Hannah gets sick so easily that her mother often keeps her home.

When Hannah was not listening, Roberta whispered to me that her mother is worried about Hannah because she has names for all their chairs. The big cushioned one is Auntie May, for instance, and the little child's rocker is Baby Lizzie. I think that is wonderful, but Mrs. Johns worries that Hannah is touched in the head.

I think Hannah just has a good imagination. Aunt Lib would probably call her a liar. Maybe she will be a writer too.

I had to leave to get home for dinner at noon. I told Roberta how I dreaded telling Mary Anna about Jasper maybe going off with a lady who thought he was too small. Roberta said I should just tell her the whole thing was a mistake and there wasn't any boy. . . . I nodded, but I knew in my heart that I could not lie to Mary Anna. So much has gone wrong for her. If she found out I had lied, she might never forgive me.

When I came into the kitchen, her eyes flew to my face. I just shook my head. She looked sicker than sick.

At dinner, I was so upset that I called Tom a jackass. Mother scolded me, of course. Then Aunt Lib said she felt Mother would rue the day she let me hobnob with a London slum child. But it is not Mary Anna who calls stupid people jackasses; it's Father. I almost said so when I saw Mother's eyes smiling.

Then Aunt Lib said, "They're subnormal. That eye colour tells its own tale."

She said it just as Mary Anna was bringing in the bowl of beef stew. Mother hushed her but Mary Anna heard, of course. Cousin Anna wrinkled up her face as though she smelled something disgusting. I keep reminding myself she has had a hard life, but it is not easy to be sorry for somebody so like a witch.

"Mary's eyes are the very same lovely green as

Cousin Margaret's," Mother said smoothly. "I've always liked it."

"Rubbish," Aunt Lib barked. But Mary Anna went out grinning.

After ten!

I just heard the clock chime. I hope Mother does not come up to check on me. She used to tuck me in, but not now that I am sharing a room. I've been waiting for Mary Anna to go to sleep and now she has. She never looks to see what I am writing, but I feel rude writing private things about her when she is awake. And I have a lot to write, dear Diary.

When we got away by ourselves tonight, I told her everything that had happened and I said how sorry I was. She gave me a strange look, her green eyes extra big. Then she said the most amazing thing.

"Victoria, my name isn't really Mary Anna."

"What?" I said. I'd heard her, with my own ears, say her name was Mary Anna Wilson.

"It's not two words. It's all one — Marianna. My mother named me after a girl in a poem."

I started to argue. Then I heard how silly I sounded and I asked her what her family called her. Her look mocked me and I could feel myself going red. She had no family around to call her anything. I opened my mouth to say I was sorry.

"Marianna or Sparrow," she said.

My eyes must have gone as round as an owl's, I was so startled.

"It was my dad's name for me when I was small. He called Jasper Scrap. Emily Rose was not born when he died. She never got a special name from him."

I felt flummoxed. Now what should I call her? I don't think I can say Sparrow unless she tells me I can. I must stop writing.

It feels strange to write "Marianna." I think I've heard that poem. I think she's the one with the broken heart who waits and waits for the man she loves to come, but he never does. I'll look tomorrow. I think it is in *Palgrave's Golden Treasury*.

After we stopped talking, Marianna turned her back and I could hear her crying. She tried to muffle the noise, but I heard. I pretended I hadn't since I knew she did not want to talk about it, and I did not know what to say.

Somehow we must find Jasper. I keep seeing his skinny little body and his red hair and his big bright eyes. But I don't know where to start.

I'm ashamed, but I also don't want to have to feel bad about it all day long. It's not my fault we don't know where he's gone.

Sunday, June 6, Early morning

I woke up early. Even Marianna is still sound asleep. Snortle has not raised his head. But I want to write about the stew because it was strange.

Mother still cooks most meals. I hate stew. The only good thing is the dumplings Mother usually makes. Well, yesterday she didn't make any.

"Where are the dumplings?" Tom asked.

Mother sank down on her chair and looked strange. Marianna had turned to go to the kitchen but, all of a sudden, she rounded on him.

"You didn't bring in the wood," she blazed. "You didn't do anything to help her. She's not well and it's too hot for dumplings."

Then she ran out of the room.

Aunt Lib's cheeks got all red and her eyes flashed. She asked if Mother was going to permit "that guttersnipe" to speak to her son like that.

Then David jumped in. "Nathan's father says the Home Children are all tainted from birth," he said. "If they had a Home Boy, he'd sleep in the back shed. Otherwise, he might burn the house down in the night."

Mother just gave David a look. It made him red in the face. I don't wonder. Then she answered Aunt Lib.

"Yes, I will permit Mary to speak to Thomas like that," she said. Her voiced dragged. "She's quite right. He didn't do his share and it is too hot for dumplings. When Mary came in, I was fetching wood for the stove. She was worried about me. My two big sons had gone off and left both the woodbox and the water buckets empty."

That was the end of that. But I saw Father giving Mother an anxious look and glaring at the boys. Even David hung his head.

What is wrong with Mother? If only it isn't consumption. But it can't be because people with that cough up blood. She doesn't cough at all. But there is some secret about her.

Later

There's going to be a concert at Trafalgar Square this week. Band music and marching. Mother says we can all go.

I told Roberta at Sunday school that I had told Marianna the truth. I told her about Marianna's right name but not about her being called Sparrow by her family. She could hardly believe it. Marianna comes to church with us, but not to Sunday school in the afternoon.

I was invited to Roberta's after Sunday school was done. I wish Marianna would stop giving me those sad looks when I come home from there. I worry about her brother, but no inspiration comes. This is not my fault.

Monday, June 7

Not only do we have the concert to look forward to, but a circus is coming to town sometime in July. A grateful patient of Father's promised to get him all the tickets we want. What fun!

"When I was a boy, we went down to see the circus train come in," Father said.

Tom and I made him promise to take us when the circus comes.

I was telling Marianna about last year when I got to touch the elephant's trunk. She was too quiet.

"Are you asleep?" I asked at last.

She said no. Then there was a long silence.

"What did it look like?" she asked finally. "I've never seen an elephant." Then she said that when he was little, Jasper dreamed of going to a circus.

"How old is he now?" I asked. My throat felt tight, but I asked.

"Eight," she said. "But he grew up fast at the work-house."

Maybe we could take Marianna with us. I must speak to Father about it when the time comes.

I stupidly asked her if they had circuses in England.

"We have circuses. They just don't take the children from the workhouse," she said, sour as a lemon. "Or from the Barnardo Homes."

I was sorry, but I felt angry too. I didn't put her in the workhouse. She's not in the workhouse any longer, nor in the Barnardo Home. She's safe with us. We're a nice family. Mother will let her go to the circus.

Suddenly, for no good reason, I remembered Father asking me what I thought of the world.

"It's a wonderful world," I told him.

Well, I know better now. It is not so wonderful for Home Children. I will stop writing and go to sleep. Snortle has been snortling for ages. It is high time to blow out the candle.

Why am I ashamed that it is still wonderful for me?

Tuesday, June 8

I went home with Roberta after school. Marianna Wilson could go home by herself, for once. Roberta and I talked about Marianna's family and how sad it is that they are separated. Roberta felt so sorry for her that she cried. She said she could not bear it if something like that happened to her family.

I was shocked. Nothing like that COULD happen to us. Her father is a stone mason. I heard somebody say he is the best builder in Guelph. Roberta's oldest brother was the one who said it, but I am sure it is true. And Father is a doctor. I can't imagine his dying but, if he did, there are my Cope grandparents, and Uncle Peter and the rest of my relatives . . .

I wonder what happened to the other people in Marianna's family. Didn't she have uncles or a grandfather?

When Mother bought her new hat at Easter, Father did say, "If you keep this up, we'll all be moving to the poorhouse." But he was teasing.

I changed the subject by asking if Lou was coming

to the concert in Trafalgar Square. Roberta said he never misses a concert if he can help it. Isn't that superb, dear Diary?

Not only that, but I heard Cousin Anna saying she and Aunt Lib are thinking about going to visit somebody else this summer. Mother says they are saving face, whatever that means. But maybe she is wrong and they will leave this week.

As Tom would say, no such luck.

I have a tickle in my throat. I hope I am not catching Marianna's cold. I am trying to keep away from Mother and not let her notice the little croak in my throat, so she won't make me stay home from the concert. You would think Father would be the one to worry about since he is a doctor but, as Mother says, "the shoemaker's child goes barefoot." Father never notices it if his children get sick.

Not only would she make me stay home, but I'd have to drink castor oil and have my throat wrapped up in a strip of camphorated flannel, which smells awful.

One funny thing happened tonight. The rain clouds blew away late in the afternoon and, just before dusk, I went out to the privy. Perhaps I shouldn't put this in but it is funny — although I would not admit that to Tom. I was so busy thinking about troubles with relatives that I did not notice anything strange. Then, all at once, there was a flip-flap-flutter above me and I looked up and saw a BAT! I didn't even stop to pull up my drawers. I dashed into the back garden, shrieking at the top of my voice. Mother came on the run and Father too. Thank heavens Tom and David had gone up the street with some friends. Mother hugged me and Father got the bat out of the privy somehow. I told Mother I would never go into that privy again.

"I foresee difficulties in your future," was all she said.

I was not going to tell Marianna. Then I could not help myself. And she laughed right out loud!

Wednesday, June 9

Mr. Grigson kept Roberta and me in tonight for passing a note. He is the meanest man in the world. I was feeling wretched all the way home, and when I got here, I was just settling down to read *Eight Cousins* when Mother made me come and help hull berries. Work, work, work! That's all grown-ups ever think about.

I could not tell her I was sick.

"Why can't Mary Anna do it?" I asked without stopping to think.

"Mary has been hard at it for over an hour. I need you too. We have all these to do yet. You'll be glad of the jam when winter comes, young lady. Now roll up your sleeves and get busy."

I sat down by Marianna but she didn't even turn

her head. Her cold is not all gone, of course, so she probably does not want to work either. And now she is angry at me for what I said. But Home Girls are supposed to do things like hull berries. That's part of their job.

I was at such a good place in my story.

If she still won't speak to me tonight, it will be miserable in our room.

Bedtime

I'm too sick to write in here, but Mother has not noticed. Aunt Lib is "feeling a bit poorly" and that takes all her time and attention. After we finished the berries, I began to shiver. Mother, who usually sees illnesses coming before they have arrived, did not notice. I was lying here half an hour ago, sure I could not write in my diary and would not get to go to the concert and trying hard not to cough, when Marianna came up with a mustard plaster to put on my chest.

"Did Mother see you?" I croaked, thinking she'd given me away.

"Of course not," she said. She did not look right at me. "Now be quiet and get well fast or you'll miss your concert."

I lay here with my chest on fire for twenty minutes and then removed the plaster. It made my eyes water and my nose run and my chest burn, but I think I feel slightly better.

Thursday, June 10, After school

Tonight is the band concert. It is terribly hot. Cousin Anna thinks maybe nobody will come.

Bedtime

Oh, the concert was glorious. Everyone was there, the Johns, even Mr. Grigson and my Sunday school teacher Miss Carter. And the music was so stirring. The military band was terrific.

But that was not what made it so exciting. We were standing listening when I saw the boy with the yellow curls who had been at the station the day the Home Children arrived. Maybe, just maybe, he would know something about Jasper. I waited until Father was completely caught up in the music and I slid through the crowd to talk to him.

"Did you get a Home Boy that day?" I asked.

He stared at me blankly for a minute. Then he remembered me and said they had.

"What's his name?" I demanded.

"Harold," he said. "He's right here. We couldn't leave him home. He's never been to a concert like this."

I was so disappointed that it was not Jasper. I was ashamed too. My cheeks burned and I thought I would burst out crying. Marianna was at home and I had not once thought about trying to bring her.

"You didn't see what happened to the red-headed boy, did you?" I asked.

"The little one called Jasper? Sure. A lady took him."

I already knew that much from the boy Roberta's uncle took in. "What was the lady's name?" I asked, new hope springing up inside me.

"I don't remember," he said offhandedly. He gave me a questioning look, as though he could not believe I was so interested in this. When he saw I was, he leaned over and asked Harold.

"Her name was Mrs. Jordan," Harold said, staring at me with serious eyes. "She didn't want to take him because he was so small. She said her brother would not want such a little fellow. But he had her brother's name on his tag and nobody else was there to take him away, so she went·off with him in the end. Her other name was some sort of flower. Lily, or maybe Violet? Jasper was crying when they left."

My heart was sad and glad at the same time. Surely we could find the Jordan place.

When we got home I waited until Marianna and I were in our little back bedroom before I said a word. Her eyes were like saucers. Well, they got very big. Eyes don't look much like saucers really.

She burst into tears and then she hugged me tight. I didn't know what to do. It's the first time she has ever touched me.

"We'll find him, won't we, Victoria?" she sobbed.

"We will, Marianna," I said, making it a promise. "Cross my heart and spit for death."

I don't know if we can, but it seemed the only thing to say after that hug. Imagine if I had told Mother about my cold! She would have made me stay home and we would never have heard about Mrs. Jordan.

When we were in bed in the dark, Marianna said, so softly I almost missed it, "When we're by ourselves, you can call me Sparrow, if you like. When nobody else can hear."

I felt like singing.

If only my throat would stop hurting!

Friday, June 11

I'm too sick to write a word but Mother has still not noticed. It is not like her.

Saturday morning, June 12

This morning I had to clean the lamp chimneys and I talked with Marianna and found out so much more. You would think the least Marianna could do would be to have hands smaller than mine so she could take over the detestable job.

I was scowling at the glass in my hand when Marianna said she used to do it in England. Then Jasper took over because his hands were smaller. Poor Jasper has my sympathy. The soot smells so sooty and I can't get my hands clean enough to suit Mother when the job is done.

Marianna did have to polish the silverware, though. And the little brass teakettle and stand some missionary uncle brought home from India. And when that's done she has to go outside and do the brass knockers and doorknobs.

Thinking of the uncle who gave the teakettle reminded me of the question I'd been wanting to ask Marianna. I told her that the brass kettle was a present from some relative. Then I said. "Do you have relatives in England? Grandparents and uncles and aunts?"

Marianna's hands stopped polishing and she gave me a long hard stare. Her eyes looked cold.

"Why do you want to know, Victoria?" she asked.

"No reason," I said, very fast. "I just wondered, that's all."

I wished, with all my heart, that I had kept quiet.

"Of course I must have kin somewhere," she said. "My mother was a lady's maid. Her family lived in Scotland somewhere, but her mistress took her south with her. They were at their country home when she met my father." Marianna stopped for a minute, then told me that her father had been a farm labourer. Her parents had very little money, but when the lady learned that they wanted to marry, she encouraged them. She came to their wedding and even gave them five pounds as a present.

It sounded like a romance in a book and I was all ears. I told Marianna so.

She said that it did not stay romantic. Times got bad and the kind lady's husband sold the farm and turned her parents out without a penny. They went to London, thinking there must be work in such a big city. They lost touch with the family back in the north.

"His folks could not write, I think," she said. "Hers thought she had married beneath her."

I forgot I was cleaning lamp chimneys. The story of Marianna's parents held me spellbound. I sat there gazing at her, waiting eagerly for the next bit.

"Close your mouth, Victoria. You look daft," she said, her mouth twitching into a sudden smile.

My mouth was hanging open. I shut it and grinned at her.

"Don't stop. What happened next?" I demanded.

She took pity on me and continued, but the laughter died out of her eyes.

Her father had an accident down at the docks which left him lame, and he began drinking to kill the pain. They had no money for the doctor. Then one night on his way home from the pub, he was set upon by a gang of thieves who left him unconscious in the gutter. They did not find him for a long time, and he died from the injuries and the cold.

"Is that what you want to know, Victoria?" she ended up.

"I'm sorry," I whispered, grabbing for another lamp chimney.

"Don't be," Marianna said slowly, her head bent over her polishing. "It feels good to tell somebody. When no one knows, you feel as though part of you doesn't exist. My mother talked of getting in touch with her family, but she never did it. I think she was too ashamed. When we were turned out of our place and had to go to the workhouse, she kept saying it was her fault. It was terrible there, Victoria. People dying of consumption. Never enough to eat. The baby got sick. It was so dreadful that my mother managed to get us all out one day and she took us straight to the Barnardo Home at Stepney Causeway."

I felt sick just hearing about what they had suffered. I asked if Mrs. Wilson had had to go back to that workhouse all alone.

Marianna shook her head and said her mother had a friend who had offered to take her in, if she was on her own. She already had six people in a room and she had no space for the three children, but Marianna's mother thought that if her children were safe at Barnardo's, she herself might get work. She had been a lady's maid, after all.

Marianna sounded so proud of her mother having been a lady's maid. Maybe such things are different in England. I cannot imagine my mother as a lady's maid. I certainly would not be proud of it.

"If she got a place, she was going to write to her family. She didn't want to beg from them after they had cast her off."

By now, we had both stopped working. She was staring at Mother's long basting spoon and trying not to cry, I think. She had been angry, but the anger sputtered out like the flame in a candle stub. It confused me. Yet I thought about it later, and I guess you can't keep your anger burning hot for years, not unless something more happens to keep it going.

That sounds like something a writer would think. Does that maybe mean I am a writer?

"That is terrible, Sparrow," I said softly, scrubbing away the tears in my own eyes and getting soot into them instead.

"I saw her once more," she whispered. "My mother. She came and looked through the bars of the Barnardo's gate just on the chance she might catch sight of us, I suppose. I told one of the women who worked there and she said it was only my imagination. If I could have found Dr. Barnardo, I'm sure he would have let me see her. But that woman gave me some errand to do and went out. We were sent to Canada three weeks later."

At that moment, Moses charged into the kitchen with Snortle right behind. I sprang to separate them before Moses turned on my puppy and gave him a swipe across his tender nose. When I sat down again, the time for talking together had passed. Marianna went off to shine the knockers. And I scooted up here to put it all down in my diary before I forget. As if I ever could!

Bedtime

Ten minutes after I finished writing and went downstairs again, Mother called in a frantic voice, "Victoria! Victoria! Run and get your father. Hurry!"

I dashed to his office and banged on the door.

"Father, Mother wants you to come quick!" I shrieked.

He was there in an instant. The two of us ran to the foot of the stairs. Mother was still leaning over the banister. She looked scared to death.

"Oh, Alastair, thank the Lord you are home," she said. "Aunt Lib has fainted or something. We found her on the floor by her wardrobe. She's moaning. But we can't understand her. Come up here. Quick!"

Father was already going up the stairs two at a time. I ran after him. I knew I would be shooed away if I went into her room, so I hovered just outside the door, listening with both my ears.

"She's had an apoplectic fit, a stroke," Father said. "She can't speak. See her mouth and the way her face is drawn down on the one side. Let's see if she can squeeze my hand. Can you squeeze my fingers, Aunt Lib?"

I could hear a sound. It was more like a moan than a word, but I think she was trying to say, "No." It was horrible, not like a person.

"How about this hand? Well, that's better, isn't it? Now you just rest a while. I know it is frightening. But

Anna is right here beside you. Lilias, step outside with me for a moment."

I ducked back out of sight behind the hall bookcase and held my breath. As you know, dear Diary, I am always getting in trouble for listening in. But I had to know.

As he came out of her room with Mother, my father spoke more quietly. He said Aunt Lib couldn't be moved and was paralyzed down one side. She wouldn't be able to talk or feed herself or walk. "I can get Graham over to take a look at her if Anna wishes, but there is no doubt what has happened."

"Poor Auntie," Mother said, her voice filled with tears.

"I think it is probably the beginning of the end," Father told her. "After all, she's eighty."

Mother sighed and said Aunt Lib was going to hate being dependent on all of us. She also told him not to bother Dr. Graham because he seemed to call by daily anyway.

"We can't cure her, but she will need careful nursing," Father said. "You can't do it, Lilias, in your condition. What about Anna?"

I peeked out and saw Cousin Anna herself coming to the door, her face shining with tears and her mouth wobbling. She looked AWFUL!

"She can't," Mother said. "She's had no training and she isn't strong."

"You are not a trained nurse either, Lilias," he

began. "Surely Cousin Anna could — "

"No," Cousin Anna whimpered like a baby. "It is all too much for my nerves."

Father gave her a disgusted look. Really, Diary, that is what it was. Then he told Mother she must not do any lifting. He said Dr. Graham had cautioned him not to let her overdo, in her condition.

"He is under the mistaken conviction that you listen to me," he finished.

When he was gone and Mother was downstairs again, I got up my courage and asked her what Father meant by "in your condition."

"Victoria Josephine Cope, stop eavesdropping. One of these days, you'll hear something that will make you a sorry girl," was all she said. "Now get busy and clear away the breakfast dishes and then give Mary a hand changing the beds."

When we were tucking in Tom's bottom sheet, Marianna said, "Don't you really know what the trouble is, Victoria?"

"No," I said, not wanting to admit it, but desperate to find out the truth.

"Your mother is increasing," she said, as if that explained everything.

I did not know what she was talking about. My face must have showed my ignorance.

"She's going to have a baby, you ninny! I don't see how you didn't know. She's worried because she's lost two since you were born."

I didn't believe her. I still don't. Babies don't come that way. Yet she says she should know, because she was with her mother when Emily Rose was born. I was so shocked that I blurted out, "Why would Mother tell you and not me?"

"I could see she was in the family way," Marianna said quietly, pretending she was smoothing every last wrinkle out of Tom's bedsheet. "I asked her when she expected the baby to be born and was the doctor worried about her. She told me the baby should come in early September and the doctor was worried because of the two she had lost. But she miscarried much earlier those times. So they are hoping everything will go smoothly."

I ran out of the room then. I didn't want to talk about such a thing. But since then I keep staring at Mother, trying to see if Marianna is right. I see now that my mother is pale and weary. Her eyes look darker and there are shadows under them. Sort of blue. But even though her cheeks look hollow, her body is much thicker. Marianna says that is the baby. It is inside her. Why didn't she tell me? Why don't people talk about it to their own daughters?

I actually brought in two armsful of wood and a pail of water from the outside pump, without being asked. I didn't even say, in a loud voice, "This isn't my job!" Well, it would be a waste because the boys are out fishing and cannot hear me. But lugging wood and water are supposed to be boys' work.

Mother smiled down at me and gave my pigtail a gentle tug.

"What a thoughtful daughter," she said absent-mindedly.

Dr. Graham came then and, after he had seen both Mother and Aunt Lib, he arranged for a nurse to come. Her name is Mrs. Thirsk and nobody likes her, although nobody says so right out loud. I think she's going to be extremely bossy. She smiles all the time, but her eyes stay cold as ice. I can tell that even Mother does not like her. She is always extra polite to people she cannot stand. Mrs. Thirsk wants to rule the roost. I actually wish Aunt Lib was well, because she would know just how to take Mrs. T. down a peg or two.

I cannot write another word. My hand is cramping. And I have a lot to think about. I keep going over and over the things Marianna told me. All that happened to her family makes me feel sick, and then there is Aunt Lib making those awful noises and Mother going to have a baby. It must feel so strange. So many shocks all at once leave me feeling muddled.

Sunday, June 13

I woke up this morning thinking this was a day like every day and then I remembered yesterday. I put my pillow over my head and tried to hide but I could not keep it up. Wish me luck, dear Diary.

Later

Sunday was Sunday, extra busy but not terribly interesting. Uncle Peter dropped by in the afternoon and asked for a bed for the night. Mother looked at him and then politely explained that we had no spare bed. And that Aunt Lib had had a stroke the day before and wouldn't he be more comfortable at a hotel.

"Don't worry about a bed, Lilias," he said, smiling away. "Your sofa will suit me down to the ground."

So he's down there on the sofa and David is in a bedroll on the floor. It is amazing what people can get away with when they are adults. He took our "No" and turned it into "Yes" without batting an eye.

Monday, June 14

No inspiration about how to find Jasper struck me in the night. Before school, we were so busy not running into each other and getting everybody fed that Marianna and I could not say one word about anything important. I admit I was a little bit glad. I had no helpful, comforting words ready.

Uncle Peter left right after breakfast, which was one mercy. Uncle Peter eats enough for two. And, of course, being a man, he does not peel a potato or dry a dish.

At breakfast Mother was so tired she scolded him for helping himself to jam with his knife instead of using the jam spoon.

"But what's the matter with my knife?" he asked.

"You get your buttery toast crumbs in the jam and . . . " she began. Then she burst out crying and left the room in a rush.

"What's the matter with her?" he asked the rest of us.

"She's expecting a baby," Father said. "It makes her touchy."

I was furious at Uncle Peter. I picked up the jampot. "Look," I said. "See the crumbs and butter."

He couldn't help seeing. He hadn't even wiped his knife off on the edge of his plate. My own uncle is a boor.

"That's enough, Victoria," Father said. But I saw his eyes gleaming. He liked my standing up for Mother even if I was rude.

And now there is no doubt about it. Marianna was telling the incredible truth. I am going to be somebody's big sister.

I wanted to show Mother that I knew all about everything. When she came back into the room I asked her if she knew when it would happen and she shrugged and said early in September, she thought. "God decides," she told me.

At school, all we do now is practise for the end of term concert. Well, most of what we do is practise. Mr. Grigson will not let me recite "The Charge of the Light Brigade." He says it is a poem meant to be said by men, and that Burt Snodgrass was going to say it. He told me not to worry.

"Here's one for you, Victoria," he said and handed me the book.

I could not believe it: "Be good, sweet maid, and let who can be clever . . . "

"I'd rather do 'Little Boy Blue,'" I yelped.

"Well, choose something yourself, Miss. But remember, the concert is only two weeks away."

I decided to find something, but tell him at the last moment so he could not change it. I wanted to shock him too. I think I have decided, but I won't write it down in case somehow word gets to him.

Tom says he will not recite, but he agreed to play "God Save the Queen" on his harmonica. Mr. Grigson wanted him to say "If" again. It is a good poem, but Tom says he is tired of keeping his head while all about him others are losing theirs.

He's not as clever as David, maybe, but he's much funnier.

After school we went to the Chalmers Sunday School Picnic. It was terribly hot. I wished we didn't have to wear so many clothes and keep our shoes on. But Nan Bryden and I won the girls' three-legged race.

We practised ahead of time so it was easier for us. The boys who won weren't a patch on us but, of course, they would not let us race against them.

Then I made Roberta go in the wheelbarrow race with me. When I was pushing her, the stupid wheelbarrow kept twisting sideways, and finally, we got laughing so hard that I could not hold it level and I tipped her out. I need not tell you, dear Diary, that Victoria Cope and Roberta Johns were not the winners.

Roberta did win the potato sack race. I might have won if I had not gotten the giggles. Giggles slow you down.

Marianna stayed home to help Mother look after Aunt Lib. I felt mean going off without her. She's never been to a Sunday school picnic. I told Father and he gave me a funny look. "Next year we'll see to it she goes along," he said.

Tom ate so much ice cream I thought he might be sick. It WAS so good!

After the picnic was over Father actually took Cousin Anna to the Sacred Concert at Knox. She was sure nobody would come and she was worried about it being a flop. Over 600 people were there!

Mr. Kelly played "The Spanish Retreat" on his mandolin. I wish I had heard that. It's one of my favourite songs.

Tuesday, June 15

Nothing to say. No peace anywhere. Told Marianna that we'll concentrate on Jasper the minute school lets out. Surely, when we have no school, and when Aunt Lib gets better, there will be more time again. I get so sick of nothing feeling normal.

Wednesday, June 16

Still no good ideas about finding Jasper. Too tired to write.

Aunt Lib is still bedridden but she is doing her best to talk. It is hard to understand her and, when you don't, she is furious.

I am learning a poem by Robert Louis Stevenson for the concert. It is so beautiful. It is a love poem. I told Mr. Grigson it was by Stevenson and let him think it was from *A Child's Garden of Verses*. He just nodded his head as though I'd said, "I'm memorizing 'Bed in Summer' or 'The Lamplighter.'" I like those poems a lot, but I am eleven and the other one is enchanting!

Thursday, June 17

Great-Aunt Lib is slowly getting better. I actually heard her try to yell at Cousin Anna this morning. I was the only one near enough to hear. I could see them, too, through the open door, although neither of them noticed me.

Cousin Anna looked down at her and said all at once, in this thin strange voice, "You are not really my mother. If you go on berating me, I am going to leave this house and you as soon as I am able."

So maybe, any day, we will be rid of one cross we have to bear.

Friday, June 18

I told Mother what I heard. She says Cousin Anna won't really go because she has no money. "We all like to eat occasionally," she said.

I told Marianna when we were upstairs. I thought she'd laugh but she didn't. She gave me one of those Barnardo Home Girl looks, priggish. "You've never gone hungry, Victoria," was all she said.

I wanted to slap her. It isn't my fault that she used to live in a workhouse. I wonder if she felt like Oliver Twist. I'd like to ask but I won't.

Victoria Cope, I did NOT feel like Oliver Twist. I felt like Sparrow Wilson with her belly twisting with the pain of hunger. Gruel or one slice of bread does not fill you. When they made us sing "God Sees the Little Sparrow Fall" I whispered swear words. God didn't love us Wilsons. If He did, my father would not have died and my mother would never have taken us to Barnardo's. Then you would not be having to live with a PRIG.

Wednesday, June 23

I am writing this in on Wednesday, June 23. My diary has been missing since the last time I wrote. I searched and searched. Finally, tonight, Marianna dug it out from under her mattress and gave it back to me. She was shaking. She read what I wrote about her last week and it made her angry.

"Mad as a hornet," was what she actually said. Then she stuck on, "a hornet looking for jam and finding vinegar."

Anyway she wrote what she wanted to yell at me right onto the page before she stopped to think. Mad hornets are given to making foolish mistakes. Then, when she calmed down a bit and saw what she had done, she hid the book away. Once she even pretended to help me hunt for it.

But we have become such friends that she could not keep it up. So tonight she gave it back and confessed. I held you, dear Diary, and I did not look at her. I read what she had written. Then I burst out with, "I'm sorry" at the very same moment that she said the same. We both laughed and cried. She says she will never write in you again. She did not say she would never read what I write again, but I know she won't unless I let her.

We are not so different.

I missed keeping a diary so much that I wrote down a few things on loose pages during the days you were lost. I'll copy them in as though I had written them into you, dear Diary. I did not write anything the first day but I began on Jubilee Sunday.

Jubilee Sunday,
June 20

I will write this on a sheet of scrap paper because I cannot find my diary anywhere. I hope Mother does not find it before I do.

I can copy things in.

Today was Jubilee Sunday. We sang ALL the verses to "God Save the Queen."

We had a guest preacher named Dr. Guthrie. Father liked what he said. Mother does not go to church any longer.

One Sunday, before she had her stroke, Aunt Lib said it wasn't seemly for Mother to be "parading herself before the congregation in her condition." Mother stiffened and Father said, "Don't get her dander up, Auntie, or she'll give birth in the pew." Aunt Lib went purple, rose to her feet, grabbed Cousin Anna's elbow and left the room in a huff.

Once she was out of earshot we burst out laughing in spite of ourselves. Even David joined in.

"I'll bet Cousin Anna still thinks a stork brings them," he snickered.

I did not tell him that lots of my schoolfriends believe in that stork. Nellie said they come in the doctor's bag. The Phillpot twins insist an angel slips in and puts them in the mother's arms. It isn't their fault. People should tell children the truth.

I wouldn't admit it to anybody but you, dear Diary,

but I used to believe the doctor brought them. I'd heard Father say he was out "delivering a baby." Well, the postman delivers parcels he brings in his bag. Why not doctors doing the same thing for babies?

But Marianna has straightened me out and promised never to let on to either of the boys.

After church, there was a parade, which Tom marched in.

Jubilee Day, June 22

Nothing happened yesterday that was worth writing down. We just seemed to work all day long. Today was Jubilee Day. Jubilee is such a glad word but all it means is that Queen Victoria has been our queen for sixty years. She is seventy-eight now. "Jubilant" must be part of the same word, but I can't imagine somebody that old being jubilant. A jubilant person dances and sings and cheers. She is nearly as old as Aunt Lib, and Auntie certainly is not jubilant, not for a minute.

We went to watch the fireworks. They were grand. For once, Marianna got to come and I did not have to feel bad about her staying home.

"She's Mary's queen too," Mother said, smiling at Marianna in a way that makes me jealous and pleased at the same time.

Just a week until the school concert. I am ready. Everyone will be surprised.

Wednesday, June 23

Now I have my diary back and can write things as they happen. What a relief! I hated writing on loose sheets and I just know they would have gotten lost if I hadn't copied them out into you, dear Diary.

Celebrating the Jubilee is grand but it makes people do strange things too. One man was stupid enough to put a firecracker in his mouth and light it for a dare. He burned off his moustache and eyebrows and half of his hair. Father read this out loud from the paper to Aunt Lib. Then he grinned and said, "I'll say it for you, Aunt Lib: There's a fool born every minute."

"How about, 'There's no fool like an old fool,'" Tom said. His eyes were sparkling.

Aunt Lib managed to sniff. But I could tell she was pleased. She didn't laugh aloud, of course, but I think she did inside.

She still is far from her old self. She seems smaller and much more feeble. Not a bit fierce.

I am too busy practising my piece to write.

Friday, June 25

I came up to bed tonight and found Marianna asleep with my old doll in her arms. She looked so tired. I was sitting on my bed staring at her when she woke up and saw me. She burst out crying.

"I'm sorry, Victoria," she cried out, jumping up to put the doll back on my shelf. "I didn't hurt her. I'm sorry. I know I shouldn't have — "

"Stop it, Marianna. It's fine," I said. But I felt confused. I don't play with Charlotte now I am eleven. And Marianna is twelve.

"I never had a proper doll," she muttered. "My father carved me one out of a piece of wood when I was little, but it didn't look human. Mother could not afford to buy me one. But I've wanted one just like yours ever since I can remember. I just meant to hold her for a minute. I didn't mean to fall asleep."

"You can hold her whenever you like," I said. I had a lump in my throat and I couldn't look straight at her. I wish she would hold Charlotte, but something tells me she never will again. I wonder what she would say if I offered to give her one of my other dolls for her own. I have four. Five if you count my old rag doll whose face is almost worn off.

I can't. I wouldn't mind, but she is twelve. I am sure she would say no and we would both be embarrassed.

Wednesday, June 30

Tonight was the school concert and I astonished them all right. So did Marianna. It was wonderful.

"Next to recite for us is Victoria Cope, if she is ready . . . ?" Mr. Grigson said.

"I am ready," I said and marched up with my knees knocking. I gulped once and then opened my mouth and went bang into it. The poem is called "Romance"

and it is by Robert Louis Stevenson. I will copy it all
out here in case I lose it or forget it in years to come.

Romance

I will make you brooches and toys for your delight
Of birdsong at morning and star-shine at night.
I will make a palace fit for you and me,
Of green days in forests and blue days at sea.
I will keep my kitchen and you shall keep your room
Where white flows the river and bright blows
the broom,
And you shall wash your linen and keep
your body white
In rainfall at morning and dewfall at night.
And this shall be for music when no one else is near,
The fine song for singing, the rare song to hear!
That only I remember, that only you admire,
Of the broad road that stretches and the roadside fire.

I wish life could really be like that when I grow up.
Imagine having a husband like Robert Louis Stevenson, who would write you such lovely poems.

I kept glancing over at Father while I was reciting.
I saw his grin. He wrote this poem out last year and
gave it to Mother on Valentine's Day. He certainly
liked it more than "Little Boy Blue." Mr. Grigson
looked red in the face, as though he was afraid Father
might think he had picked out the poem for me to
learn. He would have felt better if he knew how much

Father loves everything written by Robert Louis Stevenson. I knew he would be pleased.

When I sat back down, the surprises weren't over.

Right near the end, Mr. Grigson called on Marianna. I was amazed because she had not said a word about taking part. Up she stood, looked straight at me, winked and started in on,

> Be good, sweet maid, and let who can be clever.
> Do noble things, not dream them, all day long,
> And you will make life, death, and the vast forever
> One grand sweet song.

I almost fell off my chair laughing, but I smothered the whoops. She nearly broke down once, but she got to the end without tripping up. She knows how much I dislike that prissy poem.

A few of the people did not clap for her. David just sat there looking like a thundercloud. I wanted to kick him. But everyone else clapped twice as hard to make up for them.

July

Thursday, July 1

> No more pencils. No more books.
> No more Grigson's dirty looks.

We danced out of school. Tom actually threw away his books and then had to climb into a thorn bush to get them back. He said it was worth the scratches to see them go flying. I noticed that he didn't throw the ones he really likes. Father has told us, since we were babies, that books are our friends and we must cherish them the way we do people. He would not have cared about the arithmetic book, though.

We're going with the Johns to Puslinch Lake. I'm happy right to my bare toes. I still have to wear shoes where strangers or Father's patients can see, but that leaves lots of time to go barefoot.

David is leaving to help out on Grandpa Cope's farm. I won't miss him. I think Tom and Marianna will be pleased as well.

Aunt Lib heard me call David "you fool" once and she said I would burn in Hell for saying that. So let me just say that my brother is not a fool. He is merely an out-and-out dunce. A ninny. A blockhead.

Friday, July 2, Early afternoon

It happened! We heard something about Mrs. Jordan. We were all sitting there calmly when Cousin Anna announced she was going to visit an old school friend, Pansy Jordan.

I had a big bite of roly-poly pudding in my mouth and I choked, making a great splutter. Marianna dropped the bread knife and her face went white.

Everyone jumped at the clatter, but I am the only one who saw how pale she looked. She bent to pick up the knife and when she stood up, her cheeks had some colour again, but not much. We stared at each other. Then I swung around and stared at Cousin Anna.

"You never told me you knew somebody called Pansy Jordan," I blurted out.

Mother looked at me as though I had lost my wits.

"Why on earth would she, Victoria?" she said in a low, deadly voice. Then she asked Cousin Anna where her friend lived.

Cousin Anna said it was on a farm just south of Fergus, which is a fair distance. She said they were friends in Sunday school. Pansy's husband, Mr. Jordan, died two or three years ago, and after a while she went to live with her brother Carl.

"I've written asking if she would like a visit," Cousin Anna said. "I should get an answer soon."

"How nice," Mother said, smiling at her.

Cousin Anna smiled back, but managed to look flustered at the same time. She kept talking in a high, excited voice that sounded like somebody else's. "I never liked Carl, but I suppose he may have mellowed since we were children. I hope so. Pansy will be miserable if he hasn't. He was a cruel boy. We did our best to keep out of his way."

Her cheeks were red and her eyes sparkled. They really did. I had never heard her say so much all at once.

Aunt Lib has improved enough to be at the table again, propped up with pillows. She still can't speak clearly, and Mrs. Thirsk still has to take care of her a lot of the time. Mostly she mutters and we catch a word or two and make up the rest. Mother or Cousin Anna feed her as though she were a baby.

Mrs. Thirsk prefers to eat upstairs. She comes down, loads her tray with the best of whatever we are having, and then sails off to gobble her food in peace.

After the first shock, I watched Aunt Lib's face to see what she thought of this Pansy Jordan, but her expression was set in sour lines. She gave no sign of having heard Cousin Anna's announcement. But she so hates us looking at her being fed like a baby that her face is locked against us.

I tried to think of a way to ask what Pansy's brother's last name was, but I could not come up with a good excuse. It would be a VERY odd question. Why should I care? Once again, I wanted to pour out the whole story to Mother the minute we were on our own, but I couldn't without breaking my promise to Marianna.

That stupid promise!

Bedtime

I thought we were stumped. I should have known better.

Marianna Wilson herself managed to find out his

name. She was so smart. Right after dinner she said she had an errand to run to the post office and could she mail Cousin Anna's letter to her friend? It wouldn't be any trouble.

Cousin Anna actually smiled a real smile at our Home Girl. I think it was the first time.

"How thoughtful!" she said. It took her a few minutes to get the letter ready and we were on tenterhooks until she handed the envelope over. It was addressed to Mrs. George Jordan, Care of Mr. Carl Stone, General Delivery, Fergus, Ontario.

We were so excited. Marianna went off with it before she had finished washing the dishes. I picked up a dishtowel so Mother would not notice.

Sparrow has fallen asleep now. She was helping make jam all day and she is worn out. But I cannot sleep. How on earth are we going to find Mrs. Jordan? And how can we be sure it is the right one? Pansy is the name of a flower, it is true, but I know so many ladies named after flowers. Mrs. Dalrymple is Violet and Peggy's middle name is Rose and even Mother gets called Lily.

I'll pray about it. Mother believes prayers have enormous power. I think God must be too busy worrying about life and death matters to pay attention to my troubles, but she says He can do both. I can't understand how, but Marianna needs me to do something right away.

Saturday, July 3

Nothing new or even faintly interesting to tell. Too hot, too tired, too many chores. That is my story. When I think how I looked forward to my summer holidays! Instead of being allowed to rest after a hard year's schooling, Mother keeps piling on the jobs that need doing. David probably has it easier on the farm! Some of them are jobs Mother has always done herself before. I have discovered how deeply I hate every sort of cleaning, from washing windows to scrubbing the pan after someone has cooked eggs in it.

Sunday, July 4

Church, church, church all day.

No answer yet from Mrs. Jordan, of course. But surely a letter will come tomorrow or Tuesday. Aunt Lib is trying to talk more, but she is no nicer. When Cousin Anna spoke of her friend, Aunt Lib FINALLY got out the two words, "No . . . grit."

Did she mean Mrs. Jordan or Cousin Anna? Either way, it was mean. Then she started coughing and had to be CARRIED back to bed.

Marianna and I talk of nothing else but finding Jasper. Summer should mean more play time and it does. But you have to stay out of sight while playing or somebody will give you a task to do. I am so sick of being told that the Devil finds work for idle hands. I wanted to tell Mother that that meant SHE must be the Devil himself, since she is forever setting my idle hands to work. But I couldn't. She looks so tired.

Oh, I so hope Mrs. Pansy Jordan writes back.

We had fresh strawberry and rhubarb pie for dessert. So good!

"I need a second piece," Father said. "You haven't lost your light touch with pastry, Lilias."

"Thank you," Mother said. "But you will have to compliment Mary. She made this pie."

David was back home for the day. He looked at what was left of his piece as if he'd been poisoned. But he finished it and had another slice.

Wednesday, July 7

I know Mother wanted me to write in here every day, but I can't. Now I am feeding the chickens and helping weed the garden. On Monday I made a big mistake and pulled some poison ivy up with my bare hand. How it got growing in that out-of-the-way corner nobody knows. But I got a rash and my hand was too swollen to write with until now. My fingers looked like pink sausages. Even today, it feels stiff and itchy.

Billy Grant actually had to do ALL the weeding. He was hardly doing any before. When I told Father, he just laughed and said Billy was too old for weeding. Tom is no good at it but I have decided he just needs educating. I will stand over him and say, "Weed . . . Weed . . . Flower . . . Weed . . . " It might work.

Marianna goes to the post office every day and there are always envelopes, but none for Cousin Anna.

I took Aunt Lib up a cup of tea tonight. She couldn't hold it steady. I had to. She looks smaller somehow and not nearly so fierce. When you feed somebody by hand, it changes how you feel about them. It is as though you turn into their mother.

Friday, July 9

Cousin Anna got her letter at last and it was TERRIBLE. After all our waiting, Mrs. Pansy Jordan wrote back and said Cousin Anna must not come. She had tried speaking to her brother about it, but he told her she is needed to work on the place during the summer and can't take time to be visiting friends.

He says I am useless but he won't let me leave for even a few hours, she wrote. Then she actually said, *We have a boy to help, but Carl thinks he's worse than useless. He's only eight years old and not big for his age. Before he came, he had never seen a cow up close, or split wood or taken an egg out from under a hen. He was terrified of all of them. Carl is too rough with him but when I try to interfere, things get worse. We are both afraid of my brother. I should never have come to live with him. I knew what he was like, after all, and people don't change. Not for the better at any rate. Thank goodness he never married. His wife would have been wretched.*

Then she stopped writing about Jasper, if it is Jasper, and asked if Cousin Anna ever went to the market, because they might snatch ten minutes time together there. She brings in fresh eggs, homemade bread and vegetables on most Saturday mornings.

The boy almost always drives me there in the wagon, she ended up. *It gives us both a break. I try not to let Carl guess how much we look forward to it. I won't be there this week, but I think next Saturday we will be coming in. If you come that Saturday, I will do my best to meet you. I can't promise because Carl sometimes changes his plans at the last moment. But we might have a few minutes together.*

I know the letter by heart because she left it on the table and Marianna stole it. We read it over and over and then sneaked it into Cousin Anna's knitting basket. She'll think she left it there. It is crammed with odds and ends of things she stores away. She wants to go next weekend.

Sunday, July 11

David came home again to do some errands for my grandparents and to go to church with us. He heard Cousin Anna worrying about going to the market in Fergus next Saturday. He actually offered to drive her over there in the buggy if Father would give his permission. There's no room for Marianna or me to go too, but we will at least find out if the boy is Jasper.

David is hoping to do it so smoothly that he will win Father's permission to borrow the buggy to take his sweetheart for a ride that evening. We all know this. He'll persuade Cousin Anna to tell Father how dependable he is.

We are trying to think of some way to send a note without telling why. If this does not work, we'll have to think again. But it must work. We talked over asking David to tell Mrs. Jordan to deliver the note but, without saying it right out loud, neither Sparrow nor I trust David that far. He is still so unkind to Marianna, sniping at her, making nasty remarks about Home Children. I thought he'd change his tune by now but he hasn't. One of his friends keeps needling him about "people who give house room to Barnardo brats," and instead of being angry at him, David is ashamed of us.

I am ashamed of HIM. Imagine, Diary, having a brother who cares what that lisping noodle Nathan Cray thinks!

Anyway, we clearly can't ask him to help us get a message to Jasper. We'll have to think of something.

Can't write more now. Snortle is sound asleep and his snoring is making me sleepy too.

Monday night, July 12

Too tired to write much but I was reading over what I wrote yesterday. I remember myself thinking

once that Home Children must feel things different-
ly. I was wrong. Why can't David see?

Wednesday, July 14

The days crawled past. Lots of work and terrible
waiting for market day. It is on Saturday. I will pray
after I blow out the candle. I will even go down on my
knees in case it works better. You have to try everything.

Friday, July 16

Today in the middle of the summer, there was a
freak hailstorm in Guelph. It was not all over town,
but mostly on Waterloo Avenue. But imagine, winter
in summer!

Snortle is terrified of thunderstorms. I think he
would like me to hide in the wardrobe with him, but
I just sit on the bed with him in my arms and stroke
him and tell him to be brave.

Only one more day until we find out about Jasper!

Saturday night, July 17

Today was a tragic disappointment. I can hardly
bear to write it down.

Sparrow was incredibly clever. She sent a note with
some flowers for Mrs. Jordan. She wrote Dr. Alastair
Cope and our address on the back of a piece of paper

and talked Cousin Anna into writing a note in case Mr. Stone came without his sister. Jasper knows Marianna went to Dr. Cope's house — he was there when Father introduced himself at the station. We hoped Jasper would remember that, and recognize her writing. We also hoped he would see the note, or that Mrs. J. would just hand it to him.

But it was all for nothing.

David brought Cousin Anna right back home. She was red-eyed from weeping. The brother came instead of Mrs. J. He said she had too much work to do to be spared. When Cousin Anna said surely a couple of hours would not make such a difference, he grew rough and told her not to write to her friend again.

Marianna got me to ask David if Mr. Stone had brought his boy with him.

"I didn't really notice," David said offhandedly. "There was a skinny little brat helping unload things from the man's wagon. But I did not stop to chat."

The most surprising thing was David's anger at Mr. Stone. He said the man was horrible to Cousin Anna. It made David so furious he told Mr. Stone to mind his manners, and the man *hit* him. David has a bruise on one cheekbone. It isn't a little bruise either.

Cousin Anna shrieked at David to come away. He got back into the buggy. Then the brute struck Bess and told them to get along home and stay where they belonged.

"He's dreadful," Cousin Anna kept sobbing. "What poor Pansy must suffer! He's even worse than he was as a boy, and we were all afraid of him then."

"Was there a red-headed boy hanging around there?" I asked her after David had marched off.

"I don't know. There were some children running about. . . . Oh, Lilias, think of poor Pansy!"

"Did you find out where her brother actually lives?" Mother asked her.

"No, Lilias, I did not. You must understand I was far too upset," she wailed.

David came back, holding a wet towel to his cheek as though it were a battle wound.

"I did," he muttered "It's out past Ennotville."

He broke off suddenly, and when I looked at him his face was blank as a wiped slate. If he had started to look angry or interested or bored, he had rubbed any trace of it away before I could catch even one fleeting glimpse. I know, dear Diary. That sounds crazy. He is probably so irritated at going all that way for nothing that he wouldn't even bother telling Cousin Anna that he could find her friend for her any time he chose.

I pushed him out of my mind and Sparrow and I just stared at each other in horror. We went outside to talk and there, on the floor of the buggy, was the little basket tipped over with the wildflowers spilled on the drive. The note was gone though.

I told Marianna that Jasper might have snatched it

up. She just shook her head and I didn't try to persuade her, because I don't believe it either. The two of us just stood there, staring down at the mangled flowers. Then a breeze caught them and I pulled her away.

When we came to bed Sparrow cried herself to sleep. I felt like crying too, but part of my sadness was for Cousin Anna. She was so happy and hopeful when they set out. She is still an awful person, but I'd never seen her so happy before. And what Mother had told me about her kept coming back to me.

Father was furious too. I wonder if he'll do something. But what can he do? We should tell him about Jasper. But he heard what was in the letter Cousin Anna read out and he just shook his head.

I tried once more to talk Sparrow into telling, but she just got more upset.

"They told us at the Home that the farmers would have the law on their side," she said, "and we were to be hard workers and obedient to them and we would not have any trouble. Besides, what if we *do* tell and it gets back to that man?"

"It wouldn't — " I started to say.

She turned on me and blazed out that I was too trusting, and that if I'd heard some of the stories she has, I would change my tune. Mr. Stone might get people believing Jasper was bad and needed discipline. Then they would walk away and leave him to suffer.

"He's my brother, not yours," she ended up. "You have to do what I say."

She is right about that. I still think I should say something. But she might be right.

We were halfway through the dishes when she put in, without saying what she was talking about, "What's more, knowing that boy is my brother would make your mother sick at heart."

She's right about that too. Mother hates cruelty. She looked ill when Cousin Anna read Mrs. Jordan's words about the Home Boy.

I wonder if Marianna's brother thinks Mr. Stone's place is what Canadians call a "home." I hope we can find him and show him what a real home is.

Sunday, July 18

Today has been the worst day of my life. It started out all right. Church was as usual. It was sunny so I could watch the light shining down through the big rose window at the back. It changes the colours of women's hats. I like to play I can catch a rainbow in my hands.

After church, David went home with Grandpa and Grandma Cope, so that was one good thing.

But just as we finished our Sunday dinner and Marianna and I were clearing away the dessert dishes, there was a thunderous rap on the front door. Everyone jumped, even Aunt Lib, who seems half asleep most of the time now. It was not a friendly knock. Snortle dashed into the hall, growling like a mastiff.

Father started to go and then turned back.

"Remove this savage animal, Thomas," he said quietly. "And keep a tight grip on him whatever happens."

Tom snatched up my pugnacious pug and Father strode out to answer the door. We were all straining our ears and we heard him say, "Yes, sir? How can I help you?"

"You're Mr. Alastair Cope, aren't you?" a rough voice demanded, not at all politely.

"I am Dr. Cope," Father said in his coolest tone.

"Well, I'm Carl Stone and I want you to hand over young Jasper Wilson."

"I beg your pardon," Father said.

Marianna and I dropped the plates, without breaking one, on the hall table, and clutched each other. I think I went as pale as she did. We kept stiller than mice.

"You heard me!" the man shouted.

"I did indeed, but I have no idea what you mean. I know nobody named Jasper," Father told Mr. Stone. "And I will thank you to speak to me civilly if you must speak to me at all."

"I don't believe you. I got home last night and the boy had run off. My sister tells me that something your cousin let drop in her letter indicated that you have a Home Child named Wilson. She is the boy's sister, I have no doubt whatsoever. I don't know her given name, but she's a Barnardo Girl. I suspect you are harbouring the pair of them here, but the boy is my property under the law. I'll thank you to hand him over at once."

Marianna was shaking like an aspen. It was terrible. We both expected Father to call her, but he did not.

I could not bear just standing there. Besides, I wanted to see this monster with my own eyes. I put my finger to my lips and pulled her into the drawing room.

If we kept back, we could see into the hall from there, without them seeing us. Marianna came along with me like a big walking doll. But she had enough sense to make no sound. We hunched down behind the wing chair next to the front window and peeked out.

"Your sister is in error," Father was saying. "Since I know nothing of the whereabouts of the boy you seek and so am unable to assist you in any way, I will thank you to take yourself off my property."

The man stood his ground for a few seconds. I was so afraid he might strike my father. Father was taller, but Mr. Stone looked dangerous. His face was flushed a dark red and he was breathing hard. Then he whirled around and strode away.

"You haven't seen the last of me," he shouted. "I'll have the law on you."

Then the door slammed and Father stood very still, staring at it.

I leaned out and peered through the sheer curtains. You can't see through them from outside, but you can see out from within the house.

Mr. Stone stamped back to his farm wagon. The thinnest horse I have ever seen was tied to our hitching post. The horrible man carried a horse whip in his hand and he kept whacking it against his boot. I am sure he meant to use it on Jasper.

Father turned then, started back down the hall and caught sight of the two of us huddled by the window. He came over and faced us.

"Mary," he said, "you heard. Is your brother named Jasper?"

Marianna nodded like a puppet. I don't think she could have spoken. Her eyes seemed blind. I don't know how else to tell about their blank look. Tears began running down her cheeks but she didn't put her hand up to wipe them away.

"Do you know where he is?"

"No," Marianna whispered, lifting her chin so he could look her in the face.

"I thought not. If you hear from him . . . " He broke off, leaving the sentence unfinished. "That man had his whip ready to use on a *child,*" he said through his teeth. "He had better not come near this house again."

Mother was looking dreadful when we reached the

dining room. She had heard it all. So had the others, of course.

"I doubt the boy will get this far, Lilias," Father said gently. "You mustn't worry."

"Alastair, what if it were Tom?" was all she said.

That was when I realized that Jasper was MISSING. It takes time for things to come real when you are so frightened. But he is lost and he is just eight.

I can't write any more. Everything went on being miserable all day long. Cousin Anna kept moaning about her poor friend Pansy. She didn't care tuppence about Jasper. I care because of Marianna, of course, but also, he is not just a boy I've heard about, but a real boy I saw with my own eyes that day at the station. Maybe I wouldn't care this much if I could not see his face so clearly in my memory.

Sparrow went back to the kitchen and began struggling to do the dinner dishes. I was helping all I could. Then my wicked Snortle jumped up at Cousin Anna and made her drop the milk pitcher. Milk flooded the entire floor.

"I'll clean it up, Marianna," I said.

But I have never washed a floor. The mess got much worse when I went to work on it. Snortle tried to help me and was terribly in the way. Moses gave her tongue to the job. Then, to my relief, Sparrow burst out laughing and came to our rescue.

"I'm thinking of trying to get a position as a scullery maid," I said, hoping a joke would help.

"You need to be a Barnardo Girl to do it right," she offered.

When it was spotless, she ran up to our room and I did not follow her. I knew she needed to be by herself.

Now it is getting dark and a storm is rising. Snortle has started to shiver and whine with fear. If only somebody has given Jasper shelter. Sparrow says he is terrified of lightning.

The strange thing is that Mr. Stone did not look like a total villain except for the fury in his eyes. He just looked ordinary — his hair was fair and so was his beard, big and bushy. Yet I know he is evil. I could tell by the way his hand kept gripping the whip handle and the way his jaw jutted out. His voice too. I can't think of any words to describe it.

Noon, Monday, July 19

Last night, after I wrote that much in my diary, I went downstairs to talk to Father in the study. I told him that he *had* seen Jasper and even given him a penny for holding Bess's bridle at the station.

"You mean that little shaver with the blazing red hair was Mary's brother?" he said, staring at me.

I didn't mean to, but all at once I burst into tears. Usually Father hates what he calls "blubbering," but he just looked at me for a moment and then patted my shoulder.

"This whole child immigration scheme is open to

misuse," he muttered. "Don't fret, my honey. We'll do what we can for the lad if he shows up."

I went back upstairs and told Sparrow what I had done. I was prepared for her to scream at me, but she did not. She just stared at me and then got into bed and pretended to go to sleep.

I started to talk to her and then I was too tired. So I went to bed too. She must have really been asleep because, when I began to cry, she did not move.

I found out at breakfast that my father and Tom went out in the buggy, early, and drove down the most direct road to Mr. Stone's place. They saw nobody. He is going to take Cousin Anna out there during the day, when Mr. Stone will be away from the house. They plan to see if his sister is about and whether she has any notion where Jasper was bound.

Marianna and I can only wait and pray. It is out of our hands now. But she hugged me before we came downstairs, so that is all right.

Later

Mrs. Jordan was not home when they tried again, and they found no trace of Jasper. If he ran away, he's been on his own for two days and two nights. Will he figure out where to find us? Is he alive? Where, oh, where can he be?

I keep thinking of the hymn about the lost lamb out on the hillside all alone, "sick, and helpless, and ready to die." I always knew it was sad, but never knew how terrible until now.

Mrs. Dougal was busy at the washing, of course. What a job! Every time I watch her stirring all those heavy, steaming clothes around with her stick while her face gets red and sweaty, I understand why Mother keeps at us not to dirty our clothes. Tom's things always end up having to be scrubbed on the washboard. Boys don't realize how much trouble they are.

During the afternoon, Mother and Marianna and I were up in Aunt Lib's room, giving Mrs. Thirsk a bit of a break, when Aunt Lib managed to croak, "Boy . . . in river." Her words were garbled, but I knew what she meant to say — that Jasper had probably fallen into a river and drowned. Or that that was what he deserved.

Now I know what a scathing look is. It is what my mother gave her poor, sick old auntie. I wanted to hug my mother then and there.

"Bad blood . . . Spade a spade," Aunt Lib got out.

"That is *enough*, Aunt Lib. Hold your tongue on the subject of the boy," Mother said in a voice that froze the air it passed through.

Mrs. Thirsk came sweeping back in just in time.

"Ma'am, I think you should lie down for a rest," Sparrow said softly to Mother.

Mother smiled at her. "I'll do that, Mary dear," she said. "Don't worry too much. Most people are kind."

Then, "If you need me, Mrs. Thirsk, just call."

"I'll see to things," Mrs. Thirsk said, bustling about doing nothing. When we are not there, I know she pulls magazines and fashion books out of her bag and pores over them. It is a good thing that Aunt Lib mostly sleeps.

Mother left, holding onto Sparrow's arm. I snatched up Snortle and hugged him as we followed. I brought him in here with me and came to write in my diary. Now I will go set the table for our evening meal.

Could I be turning into a saint?

No, it's just that acting noble helps me not to fret too terribly. I think I expect God to notice how good I am and to look after poor Jasper.

After supper, July 19

I was flummoxed when I went down to the kitchen. Cousin Anna was setting the table. Sparrow had started getting the meal ready. They weren't saying much, but Marianna was looking almost cheerful. Cousin A. usually just sits pretending to knit while the rest of us work.

The day is dragging by. Writing in you, dear Diary, helps fill the time. No word of Jasper. It is over ten miles so we can't expect him to arrive at once. Sparrow thinks he would be afraid to take a ride in someone's wagon.

Bedtime

Sparrow is not herself. I know this waiting is hard for her, but there is something strange about the way she is acting. She forgave me for speaking to Father, and yet now she has stopped looking me in the eye. She seems jumpy, but not so sad. She acts as though she knows a secret. I wonder if she has some news. Surely, if she did, she would confide in me. Who else has she? I'm her only friend. She is breathing deeply now, as though she is asleep already, but I don't believe in that breathing. I'll blow out the candle and see if I can stay awake. Something is up.

Tuesday, July 20, Early morning

I was right! She did know something. I was almost asleep when I heard my dear friend Marianna Wilson sneak out of her bed and tiptoe to the door of our room. I opened my eyes a crack to watch her. She eased it open and listened. Then she sighed, closed it and returned to her bed. I went on peeking out from under my lashes and saw she was fully dressed. I kept still as a mouse and waited for further developments.

Every half hour or so, she would go and listen at the door again. At last, when the grandfather clock struck half-past eleven, she eased the door open and started creeping down the back stairs carrying her shoes.

I was up and after her like a flash. Thank goodness

Snortle was sound asleep. It takes a lot to wake up a tired pug puppy.

I trailed her down through the house and out the back door into the garden. She had left a stick holding the door open a crack so she could get in again without anyone hearing her. I left it that way too. We went along the path to Bess's stable. Then, just as Marianna's hand was on the latch of the door, my foot hit against a stone, which rolled away. Marianna spun around and stood frozen, staring into the darkness.

"Who's there?" she whispered.

I told her it was only me, keeping my voice low. "Jasper is in there, isn't he?"

He was. She was taking him food and a bottle of milk. She rushed at me and begged me not to tell the others, especially Father.

"Please, Victoria, please," she pleaded. "You can't betray him."

"Of course I won't," I promised. How could she imagine I would? I did try to talk some sense into her about letting me get Mother or Father, but she wouldn't listen.

"All right," I said. "Let me see him."

When the two of us slipped through the stable door and she lit her candle, I understood her terror. The dingy child curled up in the darkest corner was not the bright little boy I had seen at the station. If I had not known who he must be, I would not have recognized him. He is skin and bones. And so badly bruised!

I can't write about it now. Later on, when I have time to think, I will try. I know now what people mean when they talk about their hearts aching. Mine aches for Marianna and her brother.

Thursday, July 22

I didn't write any more yesterday. I couldn't. Here it is now. I'll tell it as it happened. I want to remember. It is important somehow that I put down every detail.

"Jasper," Sparrow called softly, bending to touch his shoulder.

He cried out in fear, leapt back from her hand and put up an arm to shield his face. It was clear he was expecting a blow.

"Don't hit me!" he moaned. "Don't."

"It's me, Sparrow," she said gently. "I brought you some food and an old quilt. A pillow too. Don't worry about Victoria. She won't tell. Swear, Victoria."

The boy's round eyes were filled with panic. They looked far too big in his pinched face and they burned. Mother has an old doll made of wax and its skin looks like his.

"Swearing is wrong," I mumbled.

I could tell he had a high fever. I know about fever from last winter when Tom got pneumonia and everybody thought he would die. His eyes looked just the same as Jasper's. Mother said Tom's were like "burnt holes in a blanket."

"Swear," she repeated. I could feel her glare.

"I swear not to tell," I said.

Jasper was trembling. He snatched at the bottle of milk Sparrow held out and began to gulp it down as though he were scared we would take it from him before he could drink.

I watched for a bit and then reached out and pulled it away.

"He's so thirsty. You have lots of milk in the ice chest!" Sparrow said, angry at me.

Did she really think I would not give him every last drop we had? I explained that it wasn't that. If he drank it too fast, after going hungry, he'd vomit it right back up. I've heard Mother say so. "All right, Jasper, take some more," I told him. "But try to go slowly. Small sips. There's more where this came from. I promise you will have enough to fill you up."

He stared at me.

"I know you," he said hoarsely. "I've seen you."

I reminded him that I had been at the station with Father and he had seen me then.

"You held Bess's bridle while Father talked with that woman. Then we took Marianna away. Remember?"

His eyes stopped looking so wild and he began to drink again. One gulp. One pause to breathe. One more gulp. Another shaking breath.

I stared at him. I couldn't help it. He was filthy. His hair was chopped short in ugly tufts and it was matted with dirt. His clothes weren't clothes at all. Just rags. And one of his arms looked crooked. Not the way it should.

"What happened to the things in your Barnardo trunk?" I asked, thinking of Marianna's wardrobe.

"He said they were too good for me and he had given them away to a Canadian boy," Jasper said in a flat, lifeless voice. "He told me he threw away my Bible. He said God didn't care about scum like me."

Marianna gasped. Her eyes flashed. I tried to stay calm. It was hard. Those things belonged to Jasper.

"What happened to your arm?"

"He broke it," the tired voice said, as though his shocking words were no longer a shock to himself. "He hit me with a spade the very first night. He told me to fetch the cow to the barn and milk her. I was afraid and I cried. I had not seen a cow up close and I told him I could not milk one."

He stopped to catch his breath and swallow another gulp of milk. Then his tired voice went on. He sort of droned the words.

"Mrs. Jordan wanted to take me to the doctor, but he said I was shamming. He did it to make sure I knew who was boss. I think it has just about healed up. It doesn't hurt all that much now."

All at once his teeth began to chatter and it was

hard to catch every word. Marianna wrapped the quilt around his shoulders and he gripped it tight under his chin. But the shivers were part of the fever, I guess. They kept on. They made it hard for him to hold the milk bottle steady.

I knelt down and supported it while Marianna set the candle up in a safe place. She crept out and came back with a bucket full of water.

"We'll have to wash you, Scrap," she said.

He shuddered and gave a pitiful whimper.

But I knew she was right. Mother says cutting yourself is bad, but letting dirt get into the cut is worse. He could get blood poisoning. People die of that.

We eased off the rags that hid his back and we both cried out in shock. His entire back was covered with welts, probably from that whip. Some were old scars. But many were still oozing. He must have had a terrible beating just before he ran off.

"What did you do to make him beat you?" I asked, without stopping to think.

Jasper looked at me out of those big eyes and I could feel myself shrinking down into a worm. He could not have done anything bad enough to be given such a cruel whipping.

"I stole a chunk of bread," he said. "I had to have something to eat. He'd given me nothing all day. I took it from Brutus's dish. He's half-starved too, but he let me share. Then Mr. Stone caught me. He liked hurting me. He laughed about it sometimes."

I couldn't speak for a moment because I had a great lump in my throat. Then I got up my courage and told him I was going to wash him. I promised to be as gentle as possible. I don't think he took it in. The moment I began, he gave a shriek that scared me so, I dropped the cloth. I had barely touched one of the sore places with the wet washrag. Because he was weak his cry was feeble, but Marianna clapped her hand over his mouth anyway. He hushed then.

The water did not stay clean. I went to the rain barrel for more. I was afraid the pump handle going up and down would wake someone. But no light shone through an upstairs window.

"Jasper, be still. Victoria's father will hear you and send you back," Marianna said sternly.

"He wouldn't," I said, glaring at her. How could she think such a thing of my father?

"He has to be quiet," she mumbled. "Don't talk about it, Victoria. Just get done quick."

Her threat worked. Jasper set his lips firmly and no more shrieks escaped him. He just moaned softly. That was somehow worse.

Then I realized I wasn't getting the dirt out.

"I need warm water and soap," I told Sparrow.

"I can't just go and take soap," she said, looking at the floor.

I stared at her. She had taken a quilt and food. What was the difference? Then I saw how ashamed she looked. It was because I was there and I would know. I got up and squeezed her shoulder.

"That's silly," I said, "but I'll go. I can talk my way out of it better if I get caught."

"You won't tell . . . " she started in, her head jerking up like a deer scenting danger.

"No," I growled at her and headed out the door. Why couldn't she trust me?

Then, as I lifted the latch on the stable door, I remembered what had happened to Jasper for taking bread from the dog, and I understood again how different things were for them. I had never had to be afraid like that. It made me feel dreadful.

"Victoria, I've torn up my petticoat for bandages, but we might need more," she called after me in a low voice.

"I'll get some," I called back.

There was still warm water in the big kettle left sitting on the back of the woodstove. Cousin Anna must have come down and filled her hot-water bottle. I got some soap and took the kettle with me. Then I tiptoed to where the ragbag hung and took from the bottom of it some pieces of old sheet which were so worn they were wonderfully soft.

I was so quiet I amazed myself. I even thought that when I grew up I would make a good burglar if my books did not sell. That thought almost made me burst into giggles, loud, wild giggles, but I managed not to give way. It is strange how fear can unsettle your whole body.

Sparrow had let Jasper rest and eat something while they waited for me to come back. When I eased open the stable door, it seemed to creak twice as loudly as before. I held my breath, but nothing stirred except Bess turning her head to peer at me. My unsuspecting family slept on, even Snortle.

I could not see Marianna and Jasper anywhere at first. But as soon as they were sure it was me, they crept out of the shadows at the back of Bess's stall. She was wide awake by now, and whickered.

"Easy does it, old horse," Jasper said, smiling up at her. That smile looked twisted and strange on such a small, painfully thin face. But Bess did not mind. She put her nose down to him and blew softly.

"Jasper has a way with horses," Marianna told me proudly.

Can't keep writing. Mother is calling me.

Friday morning, July 23

There is so much to tell that I am going to write part of it now and finish later. I could just put down the bare facts and do it much faster, but I want to remember all the exciting details. I somehow owe it to Marianna and her brother. And it is just like a story in a book. I want to see if I can write it the way a real writer would.

Jasper is still hiding at our place. Before we left him the other night, Marianna and I helped him up into the loft where he could hide behind the hay. But it wasn't really safe. When everyone was out or napping yesterday afternoon, I began talking them into letting me hide him in the house. There is an old storeroom in the cellar filled with trunks and broken chairs and other rubbish. Nobody goes there.

"Billy or Father will find him for sure if he stays in this stable," I said.

Just then, Jasper sneezed.

"What if you did that and they were down below?" I said.

That did the trick.

But then we had to wait hours and hours until everyone was in bed for the night before we dared try it. It was a fearful journey and I was terrified morning would come before we had him safely hidden. I was astounded when we got back to our room to hear the grandfather clock strike half past three.

But I don't see how we can keep hiding even such a small boy this way. This morning, when everyone had left the kitchen and Marianna and I were getting together a basket of food to carry down to Jasper, Cousin Anna almost caught us.

"What are you two up to now?" she demanded.

For once I was glad that she never waits for an answer. She didn't seem to notice the basket. She said Mother needed Sparrow upstairs, so I scuttled down the cellar stairs on my own.

"Jasper," I said softly.

He cringed away and stared up at me as if he had never seen me before in his life. I don't think I've ever made somebody afraid before, and it made me feel sick. His eyes looked so wild.

"Who are you?" he croaked.

"I'm Marianna's friend Victoria," I said. "I washed your sore places last night. I've brought you some food."

"I want Sparrow. I don't know you," he muttered.

He snatched at the food, but I had to leave before he had recognized me. Sparrow went down later and he didn't know her either at first. He cried out but she managed to hush him. He is really ill and I am frightened. Neither of us knows what is best to do. I tried again to get her to tell Father, but she would not listen to me. I promised, finally, to give it one more day.

"What if he dies?" I said. I did not want to, but I could not think of any other way to get through to her.

"Poor people get sick all the time and get better without doctors," she blazed at me. "Jasper's tough. Wait and see."

I opened my mouth to remind her that she herself told me of Barnardo children who had died at Hazelbrae after coming all the way from England. I am a doctor's daughter. Disease can strike down anyone. My six-year-old cousin Martha caught diphtheria last year and almost died. Two children who lived next door did die.

Then, just in time, I saw the terror in her eyes. She

knows. She just can't bear to face it.

But what will we do if he gets worse? And, if he doesn't, what will we do then? I cannot figure out where he could go. Oh, I so long to break my promise and tell Father that the boy Mr. Stone is looking for is in our cellar.

Friday, Late afternoon

Snortle almost gave us away at suppertime. He sat at the top of the cellar stairs and whined. Sparrow and I had let him come down with us earlier so that he would not whine, and he seemed to comfort Jasper. Jasper likes him a lot. Even when he doesn't know us, he pets my pup and when he drops food, because he's so weak, Snortle thinks it is a present and jumps to get it. I should have known better than to take him down there.

Tonight there is a concert in town. Father is taking me and Cousin Anna. I am so worried about leaving Jasper, but Sparrow thinks this is a good chance for her to spend time with him after she has settled Mother in bed. Mrs. Thirsk will be busy in Aunt Lib's room. When Auntie sleeps, Mrs. T. has a nap too. She snores louder than Snortle.

I hope Sparrow is careful.

My poor parents think going to concerts will make me love my piano lessons. They are wrong. I love listening to music, not practising scales.

Saturday, July 24, Early morning

Tom found out about Jasper while I was at the concert. Sparrow had gone down to check on him and Snortle began pawing at the cellar door. Finally, exasperated with him, Tom opened the door and the pup galloped down the stairs. My dear brother, being curious, followed. And scared Sparrow half to death.

When we walked in after the concert, Tom was waiting up. He doesn't usually. He kept staring at me. Then Sparrow came in and I knew something was up.

"I'm so tired," I said, yawning widely. "I'm going on up. Tom, I have that book you wanted. It's in my room."

He shot out of his chair and all three of us went pelting up the stairs lickety-split.

"Hush," Sparrow warned us. "Your mother is not well."

We tiptoed into the back part of the house, closing the door that leads to the front bedrooms, and settled down to talk. Tom was so furious at Mr. Stone, he wanted to go over there and DO something to him. Marianna begged him to be calm. Since Jasper is a runaway, she is sure he would have to be sent right back to Mr. Stone's farm.

"Don't you know that women and children have no say when it comes to things like this?" she asked, her voice hard and bitter.

Tom was angry that she could believe Father and

Mother would let such a wicked thing happen, whatever the law said.

Marianna turned on her heel and vanished. Two minutes later she was back with the paper. It told about a boy hanging himself in the barn. It said there was no problem between him and his employer, but it did not explain why a boy would do such a thing if there was no problem.

"I am certain he was a Home Boy," she said.

After that, Tom and I were quiet. After all, Jasper is Sparrow's little brother, not ours.

"Is he any better?" I asked her at last, holding my breath until I heard the answer. During the concert, I had made up my mind to break my word and tell Father if Jasper was worse.

She looked at the floor.

"He knew me . . . but only for a moment," she admitted. "But I do think his fever is lower, and he has kept food down. Just let's wait the week out, Victoria. Your Cousin Anna is talking of taking the old lady away to somebody else's house."

"Talk's cheap," Tom said, looking morose. "Who would want them? When I carried a tray up to Mrs. Thirsk this morning, Aunt Lib looked like death. Her breath was rattling and she wheezed the way I did with pneumonia. Even if Cousin Anna gets it arranged, I think Father will say she cannot be moved. And that will be that."

Little did we know that Aunt Lib was about to have

a second stroke in the night. Today she is not conscious. Dr. Graham says she does have pneumonia, just as Tom thought, and may not live out the week. Why, oh, why do so many disasters all come at once?

Pneumonia is the old person's friend, Father says. I have heard that before and I used to wonder what it meant. But I know now — Aunt Lib is so old and miserable.

Jasper is miserable too, but he is just eight. He is so much more alive, even delirious. If Jasper gets pneumonia and dies, he will only have a small part of his life, and that small part mostly unhappy. None of his dreams has had time to come true.

Tuesday morning, July 27

Two days have gone by since I last wrote. Jasper is still safe, still hidden in our cellar, still sick. But Aunt Lib died in her sleep on Saturday at about nine o'clock at night.

Cousin Anna was with her, holding her hand, but she did not wake up. Mrs. Thirsk had gone before it happened, which was nice. I was there with a cup of tea for Cousin Anna about twenty minutes before Aunt Lib died. It was horrible. She sounded as though she was drowning.

I told Father so and he said that was exactly what was happening. Her lungs were filling with fluid. I can't stop hearing the sound of her struggling to breathe, even though she is now at peace.

It is queer how much we miss her. Her special chair looks so empty.

Tuesday afternoon

When Aunt Lib died, Cousin Anna cried and cried. She has not stopped since it happened. Tom says she's a watering pot.

Mother is finding it hard to go on resting, with so much happening. If she knew about Jasper, we'd never get her back to bed. She called Anna to sit by her. I followed along, ready to listen in. What I heard actually struck me dumb with surprise, which was a good thing.

Mother started out by telling Cousin A. that she had been a good daughter to Aunt Lib. "I know she was hard on you," she said, "but now all that is over."

Cousin Anna stuck up for Aunt Lib! "Mother did her best," she sobbed, "but she never wanted a daughter. She couldn't help it that she didn't love me."

I could not believe my ears. And then Mother said something even more staggering. Aunt Lib had loved Cousin Anna and she had left her some land with a cottage on it, plus all her money.

"It isn't a huge fortune, but it's more than any of us guessed she had tucked away. She made Alastair promise not to tell you, but she did not want you to be penniless when she was gone."

Cousin Anna's jaw dropped. I did my best to disappear. I knew, if they noticed me, I'd be sent away.

"Lilias, you wouldn't joke . . . "

Mother said there was plenty for C.A. to live on in comfort for the rest of her days.

The cottage — which has three bedrooms, a parlour, a dining room and a kitchen — has been rented to some people, but Aunt Lib, knowing she was dying, asked Father to tell them she would not renew the lease.

Cousin Anna's mouth was still hanging open like a fish's.

Mother hugged her and said she would not joke about such a thing.

"You can live there, if you wish, Anna. Or you can sell it and get a place you like better," she went on, speaking gently in a slow voice. "I know. It's a shock."

There was a stunned silence. I hardly dared to breathe.

"But, Lilias, why didn't she tell me?" Cousin Anna said. She sounded as though she had been hit on the head and was dazed, instead of someone who has just learned she is an heiress.

Mother said she imagined Aunt Lib was afraid that the two of them would spend all the money and end up with nothing. By not telling, she had protected Cousin Anna's future. The lawyer would be coming to see her after the funeral, but Father and she had decided Anna should know now.

Then Cousin Anna started to cry again in great gulps and I ran away from them. I knew I was not meant to hear.

Nobody noticed me slipping down the cellar stairs before I went to bed. It made me feel a little better. Jasper knew me right away. He still looks awful, though.

I must stop writing in you for now, dear Diary. Keeping this journal is far more enthralling than I thought. I've never once been tempted to make up anything. To think I was afraid I would not be able to find anything to write about!

Wednesday, July 28

We all went to Aunt Lib's funeral this afternoon. Cousin Anna had arranged everything. There were lots of flowers. It smelled sweeter than a garden, but not as nice. I had no idea she knew so many people, but Mother reminded me that she was a preacher's wife.

Aunt Lib looked far more peaceful dead than she ever did when she was alive. But sort of frozen with an unreal smile on her lips. She looked strange without her spectacles too. I hope I don't dream about her.

The minister went on and on about what a wonderful woman Mrs. Fair had been — kind, generous. You could tell he didn't know her. He'd only come to see her twice. Cousin Anna was not at all pleased with him.

Then we had sandwiches and things and other relatives I didn't know were there, all hugging and kissing each other. They actually laughed and made jokes! I was shocked. But Mother says laughter is only crying turned inside out.

When I die, I hope they behave better. I will never understand grown-ups. I heard two ladies I had never seen in my life talking away about their false teeth.

Roberta and her mother came. When nobody was near enough to hear, she whispered, "The circus is this week. Will you be able to go?"

I did not even ask. What with Jasper hiding in the house and Aunt Lib's death, I needed to be at home.

"No," I told her. "I can't."

She looked understanding, and she doesn't even know about Jasper. Cousin Anna was supposed to be going with Father tomorrow to inspect her cottage, but she asked if he could possibly take her today. It was already after four o'clock and everyone was surprised.

"But, Cousin Anna — " Mother began.

"Don't say no," Cousin Anna begged. "I couldn't settle down to anything and I cannot wait another day to see it."

She sounded like me on Christmas morning.

So off they went. Mother had sent Mrs. Dougal and a friend of hers to go in and clean it after the renters left. I wonder what it is like. If I weren't worried about their finding Jasper when I'm not home, I would have asked to go along for the ride.

Later

Father came home alone. Cousin Anna wanted to stay overnight.

"But, Alastair," Mother cried, "what if she wakes up all by herself in an empty house? I'm quite sure she's never spent a night alone in her life."

"Perhaps that is why she has chosen to do so now," Father answered.

David had come home for the funeral and he offered to go over and keep her company. I think she'll be glad to see him. Father said he could walk over after supper, but not to push himself in if she did not want him.

Our house seems incredibly quiet now. Even Snortle notices and tries to find everybody.

"Poor little fellow, trying to run us all to earth," Mother said. "Calm yourself, Snortle. The peace won't last."

Moses is not her usual self either. I've never felt like this before. It is like being lost and yet knowing you are foolish because you are still in your own house.

Thursday morning, July 29

Wearing dark clothes all the time makes me dreary. Mother won't put a child in black, but she is wearing it herself and it makes her look like a ghost.

Jasper is definitely better. He knows us now. But we

will soon have to make a plan. He can't spend his life in the cellar.

Tomorrow, while Mother is resting and Father is making his house calls, we are going to let him come upstairs for a while so he can see the sunlight and not feel like someone shut up in a dungeon.

Goodbye for now, my dear Diary, keeper of my secrets. I have never had so many secrets in my life before.

Friday, July 30

Today was a catastrophe from start to finish. I can't bear to write it. Jasper has run away!

It was all that Mrs. Jordan's fault.

No, it wasn't. I know whose fault it was. Mother was resting and had fallen fast asleep. Father had gone out on a baby case. Mrs. Dougal went home early because her sister had come to visit from Niagara Falls. Cousin Anna was still at her cottage, and of course Mrs. Thirsk hasn't been here since Aunt Lib died. So I, clever Victoria, had this great idea to bring Jasper up out of the cellar so he could get some light and air. It seemed perfectly safe. He must have been looking out through the front room window when Mrs. Jordan drove up in her buggy.

He gave a shriek and we ran to see what was wrong. There she was tying her horse to the hitching post. We trusted Jasper to go back in hiding. Tom and

Marianna and I had a quick consultation while she was coming up the walk. Then we met her at the door.

We were worried about her seeing Jasper, so we did not invite her in. I just spoke as politely as I could, and told her Cousin Anna had gone to her cottage on Paisley Road.

"Oh," she said, staring at me. "You mean she's out?"

I had to explain about the cottage because she knew nothing about it, of course. She said a few more things — talking to herself as much as to me — enough for me to realize that her brother went off somewhere for a couple of days and she made up her mind to leave. It sounded as if she just packed her clothes, hitched up her horse and buggy, loaded the clothes onto the back and, when Mr. Stone left the house, set out for Guelph.

And now that she knew Cousin Anna had her own cottage, Mrs. Jordan decided she should go there.

"Carl will never dream of looking for me there. He knows about this place, you see, but he has no idea Anna would be somewhere else," she trilled, her eyes sparkling. "He is still in a rage about that little Jasper Wilson running off. He'll be angrier yet to discover I've gone. So he must not find me."

"Oh," I said, trying to keep my face blank. "Hasn't that boy come home yet?"

"No," she said, giving us a strange look. "As a matter of fact, I thought I saw his face at the window when I was tying Minnie to the hitching post."

"No," we all shrieked, as though she had accused us of some terrible crime.

"It must have been our other brother you saw," I said, thinking fast. I was proud of myself. And Tom, also inspired, said he could show her to Cousin Anna's cottage if she liked.

At last they were out of sight. I was pleased Jasper had been smart enough to slip away without anyone noticing. I took it for granted he was back in the cellar. Marianna and I dashed down to reassure him.

Nobody was there.

We hunted high and low. It was terrible. No Jasper anywhere.

"He must have seen her," Sparrow moaned. "He should have trusted us. Oh, Victoria, what will we do?"

I told her to keep looking. I could not believe he had really vanished. But we could not find hide nor hair of him. He seems to have disappeared off the face of the earth. Well, that can't be true, but it feels that way, and the three of us are so afraid for him.

He was smart not to go back into the loft, of course, since Mrs. Jordan's mare might have been stabled there overnight, if she had ended up staying. Maybe he is watching the place and, once he is sure she is gone, he will creep back. Sparrow is beside herself, but I tell her to keep hoping.

If only Mr. Stone stays away until Father comes home. If only Jasper turns up unharmed.

Tom came back first, of course. He said Cousin Anna and Mrs. Jordan were like two schoolgirls, they were so excited about meeting again. They hardly noticed when he left. He asked if they needed anything.

"No, no. You run along, Tom, and tell them we're as happy as two kittens in a basket," Cousin Anna told him.

It doesn't sound like her, but Tom swears that is what she said, word for word. Father did come home too, after I had almost given up on him. He was so pleased about the delivery — twins — that he did not notice anything out of the way.

I wish I had seen the meeting of Cousin Anna and her dear friend Pansy. It would be a good thing for a future writer to observe.

Now I am going to bed.

If only everything would be ordinary for a few days. I'd like to go over to Roberta's house and play dolls and forget about people being poor and sick and dying.

Mother is not well. Sparrow has just told me that she is really worried about her. She has been resting when she can and taking her tonic, but it has not helped. Father has asked Dr. Graham to come back tomorrow.

Please, God, let my mother be all right. Nothing else matters.

Except Jasper. Please, Heavenly Father, find him for us and let him be unharmed.

Saturday afternoon, July 31

Mother has to stay right in bed from now until the baby comes. Marianna told me that Mother's legs were terribly swollen and she is often dizzy. The doctor had not come for a few days and he took one look at her and told Father if he didn't want to lose another baby and perhaps his wife as well, he would see to it that she stayed in bed from this moment on.

"If I did not know you had had a death in the family, I'd have a few harsh words to say to you, Alastair," he told Father. "Lilias is in real difficulty. Take care of her and see that the rest of your brood does, too, if they want to keep her."

Marianna told me that Father looked scared. I know I was terrified at hearing what Dr. Graham said.

He and Father brought a bed into the dining room so that Mother would be close enough for us to watch over her. They raised the foot of the bed up on bricks so poor Mother's on a slant. She has a pillow under her head, but the rest of her slopes up to her feet. He told Marianna certain foods to give her. Lots of fruit juice and milk and beef tea. Calf's foot jelly.

I stood in the hall listening with both ears, and watched Sparrow nodding her head up and down, up and down. I could see her hand patting Mother's shoulder while she took in all the orders.

"You are a sensible girl," Dr. Graham said at last, smiling at her. "I believe you have had some experience of birthing babies. Am I right?"

"Yes, sir," she said, calm as a cucumber. "Before my dad died, I used to go along with my mam to help out. She was the midwife in our neighbourhood."

"Well, we don't need you to deliver this baby, but I do want you to follow my instructions to the letter. If Dr. Cope is not home and you think I should be called, send one of the children. Alastair, you make sure that they will do what she says."

"I will see to it. I think they would in any case, if they knew their mother needed you," Father said.

"I don't know how they'll all manage without me," Mother said feebly.

But even I could hear the relief in her voice as she let go of the job of keeping the whole family going.

Sparrow is calling me.

Saturday Evening

I am going on with my diary while Mother sleeps.

Dr. Graham offered to ask Mrs. Thirsk to come back.

"Mrs. Dougal and Victoria and I will manage just fine," Marianna said firmly, and I agreed in a loud voice. Father had to go to his office. The waiting room was filled with impatient patients. He told Tom and me to do whatever Sparrow said.

"You don't need to tell me," I blazed.

"I know, Vic," he said gently, patting my shoulder.

To tell the truth, I was so frightened I could hardly get the words past my lips. How could we manage? Even with Mrs. Dougal here through the week, I was really quite sure we could not. I can dust and lay the table and wash and dry the dishes. I've helped make griddle cakes and I can make tea, of course, and boil eggs. I can make toast with the toasting fork and never let it burn. But nobody has taught me to cook, not whole meals for a family.

Marianna looked at me and grinned.

"We can do it," she whispered. "You'll see, Victoria Josephine Cope."

She was at the helm and she sounded as though she knew exactly where we were bound and how to get us there. She didn't leave me time to fret. She sent Tom off to the grocer's and the chemist's for supplies. Then she told me to go and keep my mother company.

When I tiptoed in, Mother looked hot and fretful and not like herself. Then Sparrow came up behind me and pushed a palm-leaf fan into my hand.

"Use this to help cool her," she said softly. "I'll bring you a cloth and some water for wiping her face with. But don't pester her. And don't chatter, Vic. She's tired."

So I sat and fanned Mother and wiped her forehead with cool water. And, much to my surprise, it seemed to help. It was a good thing Marianna warned me not to talk, for I was about to start jabbering to keep her entertained.

"Maybe you should sing me a lullaby, daughter," she murmured. I thought she was teasing until I saw her eyelids drooping.

I began to sing softly some of the songs she used to sing to me when I was little. "Lullaby and Good Night" and "Sleep, My Child, and Peace Attend Thee." Then I thought of Christmas carols and started in on "Away in a Manger" and "Silent Night." They made me feel cooler and they put my weary mother to sleep. I was so proud when I heard her breathing grow slow and knew she had gone to sleep.

The moment I relaxed, I remembered that Jasper was still missing. I wonder how Sparrow keeps going so bravely. I suppose she has had so many hard times that she has worked out ways to get through them.

I asked her if this was true.

"You'll soon see, Victoria, that hard things are easier to stand if you keep busy," she said.

I wonder if that is true for everyone or just for Marianna Wilson.

She made mock duck and cottage pudding for supper. She also set bread to rise. Then she left me in charge and went over our house and property again, in case Jasper had crept back. He had not. I knew by one glance at her pale face.

When Mother woke she automatically began to get

up, but I pushed her back on her pillow.

"Rest, Mother," I commanded her. The words came out in a hoarse croak which I could not keep steady. "Marianna Wilson has everything in charge. You are NOT to stir."

"And you, my honey, are her right-hand girl," she said.

Then Sparrow came with the commode and helped Mother get to the chair to relieve herself. I had forgotten that. Then she brought a basin of warm water, soap and a towel.

"Victoria, toast her a slice of bread with honey on it and make her a cup of weak tea," she commanded me.

I ran. It was comforting to have someone telling me good things to do for my mother. I made the toast exactly the way she likes it, not too dark, not too light, just golden.

Father came and discovered her half-asleep. She smiled at him.

"You look better, Lilias," he said softly, "thanks to these three wonderful children."

It was strange. Marianna did not seem a child to me.

Then and there, I told them the truth about Marianna's name. After all, Cousin Anna was not in the house all the time any longer. They were amazed. I didn't tell them her nickname, though. They will hear Jasper saying it someday, I hope.

"Marianna, you should have told us," Mother said.

Marianna just looked at her.

I remembered then Mother's telling her we would call her Mary. It seemed as if that long-ago Home Girl was not this girl, but someone different.

Bedtime

Cousin Anna dropped by for a few minutes before it grew dark this evening. Mrs. Jordan drove her in the buggy. She came to get some more of her belongings — David had already taken over her small valise — but seeing Mother in bed filled her with guilt.

"Victoria, get her out of the house," Sparrow hissed into my ear. "She'll wear your mother out."

I was paralyzed for a moment. Then I marched in and drew Cousin Anna out of earshot of her friend.

"Mother will be fine, Cousin Anna," I said solemnly. "We are all here to help. But you must go back to your cottage and keep Mrs. Jordan safe from her brother. He's been here, you know. He frightened me. And he'll be looking for her."

I could not think of anything to add, but I had said enough. She was out the door like a flash.

"Well done, Victoria Josephine," Marianna said, grinning a tight grin.

Then Tom said, "Vic, you take the first watch."

It was right out of the sea adventure books he loves. He sounded excited, pleased to be doing something real. I know how he feels.

Mother is not to struggle upstairs any more. Father put a screen around her bed to give her more privacy, and we'll eat in the kitchen. She had some soup and toast and went back to sleep. I sat watching her, and Marianna kept creeping back to check up on me. At eleven, she took my place.

I am back now in my own room. And Marianna Wilson, to her own astonishment, will have a room all to herself. David is coming back home tomorrow. He'll get a shock to find Mother sleeping downstairs.

Moses is also keeping watch. She is lying very still at the foot of Mother's bed. I went to shoo her away but Mother said sleepily, "No, Victoria. She is teaching me to relax."

I must sleep now. I go back on duty first thing in the morning. I thought at first that Sparrow was being silly to have one of us with Mother all the time, but when she needs the commode or a drink, she won't "bother" us. She is up before you know it. And Dr. Graham said no getting up at all.

August

Sunday, August 1

It did not feel like Sunday today. It was strange.

No word of Jasper. We don't speak of him, but I see the fear in Sparrow's face whenever she thinks nobody is watching. She still won't give in and tell Father. I know it is because she is afraid Father would be bound by law to return Jasper to Mr. Stone. I am sure she is wrong, but what if I were the mistaken one?

Bedtime, Monday, August 2

Thomas found Jasper!

He went fishing. Mother said she wished he would catch some fresh fish. She had a hankering for it. I think maybe she was just trying to cheer him up but maybe not. Off went Tom like a knight answering his lady's behest.

And we waited for him to come home quickly, because he's a good fisherman and he always catches at least one or two decent-sized fish. But he didn't come. We had supper. Father had a meeting at the church, so he was not home. Sparrow and I were just getting anxious, when Tom came. He looked so smug I wanted to hit him.

Waving a fan for what feels like hours, while you yourself are melting from the heat, is tiring. The room was so hot and I had to keep the light dim and stay awake and pretend I was enjoying myself. Even when Mother drifted off I had to stay there in case she woke, and because of no light I couldn't read. I was glad to do my part, of course, but even so it was no fun.

And I believed Tom, the lucky fellow, had spent

the day lolling by the river Speed, never giving a thought to us. I glared at him when he waltzed in.

Then he beckoned to Marianna and me. Sparrow looked as annoyed as I felt, but we followed him. He led us out to the stable and there was Jasper! He lay in a huddle in Bess's stall and he was asleep.

Sparrow actually hugged Tom. He went red as a tomato.

"Where was he?" I demanded in a whisper.

He looked terrible. Filthy dirty. All his bones showing. Several new bruises. Sores around his mouth.

But alive!

Tom said it was a miracle. He decided to try fishing in a new place. He went down Norwich Street and sat on the bank near the bridge. Jasper was hiding in the bushes under the bridge supports. He saw Tom but he waited a long time to make sure Tom was alone.

Jasper figured somebody in our family had told Mrs. Jordan where to find him. He thought it was Cousin Anna.

"I told him she was dotty, but not a lowdown skunk," Tom said, keeping his voice down.

When nobody joined Tom, Jasper took courage and called to him.

"What did you do?" I asked.

"I nearly jumped out of my skin," Tom admitted, grinning and rubbing the back of his neck. "He sounded like a ghost."

Then he said they would have been home long

before but Jasper would not leave his safe hiding place until it began to get dark. He'd only ventured out once, to scrounge some food. Tom wished he'd had some bread and cheese with him — for himself as well as Jasper. He said he felt as though he would die of hunger before Jasper gave in and came with him.

Sparrow ran to get them both something to eat, taking with her the two smallish fish he had caught. Mother would be pleased with the fish, and the story too if only Marianna would let us tell her.

"You know, Vic, I did not promise not to tell," Tom said into my ear. "I think it is time to get help. That kid is really sick, or I miss my guess."

I agreed, but I HAD promised. I wished Tom had told without discussing it with me. We sat in the stable yard, where Jasper would see us the moment he woke up. We did not want him to be frightened and we wanted to make sure he stayed put. I thought it would be all right to leave Mother for those few minutes.

"It's a good thing Billy's gone home," I told Tom. He nodded.

While we waited there I told him all Mother had confided to me about Aunt Lib and Cousin Anna long ago. Now that Aunt Lib had passed away, there was no reason to keep that secret, at least. When he heard Cousin Anna was not Aunt Lib's daughter, Tom was as dumbfounded as I had been.

"Jumping Jehosaphat!" he yelped out, exactly as I had done.

Then he told me that he used to plan he would someday run away to sea.

"No, Tom," I said. "You mustn't."

"I know it, goosie," he said.

Then I burst out crying and he said go ahead and cry. I think he cried a little himself. We are both so worried about Mother.

"I wish Marianna would bring that food," he started to say when, all at once, Father came walking down the path.

"What are you two in cahoots about?" he asked.

His deep voice half-roused Jasper, who cried out, "No! I won't go back. I won't!"

Then all the hiding was at an end.

Praise God from whom all blessings flow.

I'll write the rest in the morning.

Tuesday, August 3

There is so much more to tell about yesterday. My hand aches just thinking about it. But it makes a grand story.

Just after Jasper gave himself away, Marianna came flying back down the path with food for poor Tom. She had been held up by Mother, who had asked her help with something or other. Father looked down at Jasper, who had gone right back into a troubled sleep, and made a sound like a low moan. He leaned down and touched Jasper's head with the back of his hand.

"Poor laddie," he said softly, "you've a fever. Some devil has been thrashing you. Mr. Carl Stone, I warrant."

He drew us back outside, and while Tom ate, Marianna and I poured out Jasper's story. Father looked terribly angry, but not at us.

He told Marianna that she need not worry. Mother would want to know. He explained that she needed to rest her body, not her mind and heart. When Jasper moaned again, Father went back in, lifted him very gently and carried him up the stairs. Marianna heated water and filled the tub and Father himself washed Jasper. He said he had to be sure each wound was thoroughly cleansed or we'd have a case of blood poisoning on our hands. He carried Jasper as though he were light as a feather, and when I took an old nightshirt of Tom's in to put on him I saw why. All his bones showed through his skin. I could have counted every rib and backbone bump. His shoulder blades are so sharp that they look like real knife blades. He was so filthy that we had to empty the tub and fill it with clean water twice. Before it was washed, his hair showed no sign of being red, only dirt-coloured. I stood gazing at his poor wasted body in horror.

"Victoria, stop staring," my father said. "Leave the young man some privacy."

I went red then and hurried out. But to tell the truth, I had not seen him as a boy but only as a skeleton. Besides, he's only eight! If he were my age,

I would never have stayed.

I hate that teasing smile of Father's. I blush even when I am not really embarrassed at all.

Now Jasper is in my old bedroom, so I had to move again. Tom has moved back into the front room he and David shared when Peggy lived with us. Cousin Anna moved out just in time.

When Marianna fed her little brother the food Father prescribed, he ate like a starving wolf. She kept making him stop gulping long enough to chew. It was hard to watch. Yet it was wonderful too. It was like seeing a plant dying of thirst get watered and begin instantly to revive. A chewing, gobbling little boy does not look like a corpse.

Before Marianna tucked him in, Father took him to meet Mother. I went along, bound and bent not to miss anything. She looked at his thin, bruised little face and began to cry. His face is not just thin. It is gaunt, I guess, or maybe haggard. It looks like a skull except for the blue, blue eyes and the anxious smile. His hair, now it has been washed, is almost as bright as it was that day in the station, even though Mr. Stone has chopped a lot of it off.

"Come here, Jasper," Mother said and gathered him as close as she could manage. She has no lap with that baby taking up space. She whispered something into his ear. Then he had tears in his eyes too. We were a bunch of watering pots.

I wonder what she said. He might tell Marianna. It

is not my affair, but I would so love to know.

"We'll talk this all over in the morning," Father said when Marianna had put Jasper to bed. "We have things to work out."

Tom and I avoided his glance, sure we were in trouble.

"Nobody shall ever lay a finger on that child again if I can help it," he called after us. "You did well, my children."

"Yes, Father," Tom and I mumbled and made our escape.

Then Snortle came in and jumped up at me, wanting a share of the attention. I picked him up and scratched behind his soft ears. He is getting heavy! Thump, thump, went his silly tail. So blessedly normal!

He washed out my left ear with his soft tongue while I headed for my room and you, dear Diary. It was a huge relief to laugh.

What a strange day! What a blessing that Father now knows! Maybe I won't have any bad dreams tonight.

Wednesday, August 4

David came home late last night. Nobody told him about Jasper. Maybe we wanted not to have to listen to his sneers. But I don't think that was really it. I know this sounds incredible, but David seems like an outsider now, and I forgot that Jasper's being here had anything to do with him. I really did.

Mother told him that, now Cousin Anna was in her cottage, the front room was free for Tom and him again. She said nothing about my old room, but David did not notice that. He doesn't notice things having to do with other people.

"Feel my muscle," he told Tom, flexing his arm.

Tom felt it.

"That's impressive," he said.

We did not get together and decide to keep Jasper a secret. But none of us said a word about him either. He was quiet and out of the way and David was leaving again before long. Maybe we thought the less he knew, the fewer mean things he could say.

But it was a mistake. Halfway through the morning, David needed a clean towel and went to the linen cupboard. It is between my old room and the little one Marianna and I shared. I was in the kitchen when I heard his feet stop outside Jasper's door. Jasper was asleep, but every breath he takes rattles and wheezes. I had just been up to check on him and I had heard this from outside the door. So I held my breath and prayed David would not notice.

He clattered down the back stairs like an avalanche. Then he just stood and glared at me.

"Who is that kid?" he demanded.

I had totally forgotten that David had never even heard of Marianna's brother, let alone seen him. I was so taken aback my mouth dropped open. I felt it drop. Then I answered like a ninny.

"Jasper," I said.

"And who, pray tell, is Jasper? I've never laid eyes on him and he is wearing an old nightshirt of Tom's and looks settled in for life. Am I a member of this family or am I not?" He forced the words out like the bits of meat squeezing out of the grinder.

Marianna came in with some vegetables she had just picked for dinner. She saved me having to answer.

"He's my brother," she said, her voice thin. "I'm sorry you didn't know about him, but we've had to keep him a secret or he would not be safe."

David's face darkened and his eyes narrowed. It changed him into a stranger. He looked like what Father calls "an ugly customer."

"Awww," he drawled, mocking her. "That explains everything. Are the police after him? He looks like a little roughneck. Jailbird haircut and everything. I certainly wouldn't trust him out of my sight."

I started shouting at him before Marianna had a chance. "Jasper's only eight years old! He was beaten by Mr. Stone. He was starved too. He ran away and found Marianna. He needs nursing."

David gave me the nastiest look. A sneer. That was what it was. Then he said he was sure that Father did not know we were hiding a runaway Home Boy in the house and he was sorry but it was his duty to tell. He sounded not one bit sorry, just pure mean.

Then, dear Diary, just as I was about to fly at David, Father came striding into the kitchen where the three of us were getting set to do battle.

He said he knew all about Jasper, and that Mother was not well and David was upsetting her. Then he told David to take himself off and not return until he had come to his senses. He finished with, "What becomes of Jasper is no concern of yours."

David opened his mouth to argue, but Father turned away and said he had to go out on country calls.

"I won't wait to eat," he told me and Marianna. "They will doubtless ply me with food."

At the door he turned back and asked David if he'd like to come along. I was amazed by how calm he sounded, and even more amazed when David muttered he had something else he must do. We all love to go with Father on his country calls. He takes only one of us at a time, and we get a chance to talk with him without anyone else butting in.

Father was pulling the door shut behind him when David burst out, "Having that boy in the house can't be good for Mother. He must be crawling with vermin and — "

"He is not!" Marianna spat the words at him.

"Enough, you two," my father said. "I helped bathe Jasper, David. You must admit I know how to get a small boy clean, even if he is bruised and battered."

Then he really left, shutting the door firmly.

"I'm going downtown," David announced loudly and slammed out.

Everything is ready for our noon meal now but we are waiting for Tom. So, dear Diary, I am getting caught up.

Wednesday evening,
Written by the light of a candle,
Sitting by Mother while she sleeps

I had no idea when I wrote those words what was hanging over us. I actually saw David go by the window on the bicycle Father and Mother gave him for his last birthday. I was surprised he was riding it just to get downtown. I should have paid more attention. He was not going into town but out.

He returned long after we had finished dessert. He looked from one to the other of us. He seemed about to speak, but didn't. He went upstairs and did not come down. The afternoon was peaceful.

Then Snortle barked to tell me company was arriving. I went to the door. I looked out and froze. Climbing down from the seat of a farm wagon was Mr. Carl Stone. I could not move hand or foot for a few precious seconds. It was as though I had been turned to stone, dear Diary. I could not make my brain work until he spoke.

"I've come for the boy," he barked.

I stood there, like a life-sized statue of a girl with

her mouth open. I was blocking his way, but not because I had thought it out. I couldn't seem to think.

"Are you simple-minded, girl? I know he's here," he said, raising his voice as though I were deaf. "Your brother did me the courtesy of riding out to tell me you had him. Tell Jasper Wilson I am waiting and he'd better get out here fast if he doesn't want a hiding."

I knew Sparrow was running up the back stairs to warn her brother. Maybe she could even hide him. David was staying out of sight. Father had not yet returned from his calls. It was up to me and I was scared stiff. Mr. Stone had his whip in his hand again and I thought Jasper was lost.

Dear Diary, I was in dark despair.

Then I heard slow steps coming and Mother's voice spoke from behind me.

"My husband is not at home, Mr. Stone," she said clearly. "Would you come into the sitting room and wait for him please?"

He did not want to. He grew as red as a beet. Mother was in her nightgown with a wrapper over it and her hair was hanging down her back in a long plait.

"I'm dirty from the road, madam," he growled. "All I want is Jasper Wilson. I have papers which prove he was signed over to me until he is eighteen. He had no business running off and snivelling to you people about being mistreated. He's only been punished when he richly deserved it."

"You will please follow me," Mother said.

She turned slowly, looking more like a sailing ship than ever, and walked into the parlour. There was nothing he could do but follow. As she shut the door, she gave me a look that said she was counting on me to make certain that, when Mr. Stone came back out to search for his Home Boy, Jasper would not be there for him to find.

I raced up the stairs. Sparrow was dressing her brother, shoving his arms into an old shirt of Tom's.

"Mother's got him shut up with her in the sitting room," I said, gabbling the words so fast it was amazing they understood me. "Oh, Sparrow, what can we do?"

"I don't know," she said. "But Jasper can't go anywhere in a nightshirt."

Then I was inspired. The Johns would help! Roberta had been in on the whole story, and I knew she had told her mother about Jasper. Her mother had tried to get Roberta to tell more, but Marianna had pledged her to secrecy before sharing the story. I could not ask my mother what I should do and so, for the first time in my life, I decided what we should do next and saw to it that Tom and Marianna helped me.

We sneaked Jasper down the back way, without a sound. I scribbled a note to Roberta's mother explaining what had happened. Then Tom lifted Jasper up onto his bicycle. Jasper was reaching out for his sister and tears were spilling down his poor hollow cheeks.

"Mr. Stone is in there. Hold on, Jasper. We must ride like the wind if we are to escape the evil tyrant," my clever brother said into the little boy's ear.

Then they were off, heading for Roberta's house, with my note explaining everything tucked into Tom's pocket. Thank goodness the drive does not go by the parlour windows. They passed Father coming up the side of the house. He stopped to stare. I ran to meet him.

"Mr. Stone is in with Mother," I told him breathlessly.

"How on earth did he find out?"

I hesitated, but he had to know some time.

"David," I said over a lump in my throat. "He rode out there and told him."

Father looked sick. I hope I never in my whole life make such sadness come into his eyes. Then he hurried into the house.

Mother and Father between them got rid of Mr. Stone, although he insisted on searching the back bedrooms. David must have said Jasper was in one of them.

"Our Home Girl sleeps up here," Father told him in words that sounded chipped from the blocks of ice the man brings for the ice chest.

I can't write more now, dear Diary. I have to go to sleep. The house is filled with worry. Nobody is speaking to David. He tried to say he did it because Mother was sick and needed all Marianna's attention.

Mother just looked at him.

171

"Oh, David," she whispered. "Don't."

She had tears on her face and Sparrow took her back to bed. I'm crying now. Tomorrow we will have to go over to Roberta's. It feels as though I used to have a whole family, and now it is broken.

Thursday morning, August 5

I think the baby is coming. Mother started having pain. Father almost took me over to stay with Cousin Anna, but Marianna told him I should stay right here where I could be of help.

"My mam said all women should know these things," she said to him. "It's her right. She's no infant." I don't know what she meant, but he looked at me and then nodded slowly.

"Very sensible. Do whatever Marianna tells you to," he said.

I am getting tired of being told to obey Marianna. I would anyway. Mother began having her pains in the night but they seem to come and go. In between she talks to me and looks like her ordinary self.

I wish I knew what to expect. I can tell you, dear Diary, that I am afraid.

Early afternoon

The doctor came. He has been here most of the day. Mother's pains stopped and did not start again. The baby is coming a couple of weeks early. Marianna said Mother was not expecting to "go into labour" until the end of August. Will it hurt the baby if it comes too soon? Nobody tells me anything.

"Go into labour" sounds strange.

"The baby's just taking a rest while he gathers up his strength for the big push," Dr. Graham said. "He knows he might have his work cut out for him."

"*She* knows," Mother said faintly, smiling a tiny smile at me. "Victoria wants a sister."

Dr. Graham chuckled.

"We'll do our best," he said. "But she's putting in her order a little late in the day."

But his eyes were not laughing. Is he afraid? Does he know something terrible? Joan Macgregor's mother died having her little brother. I wish I had not remembered that.

Friday, August 6

Today began as another day of waiting. I felt as though I were going to explode and fly about the room in little screeching bits. Then Mrs. Cameron came over and sat down next to my mother.

"Victoria Cope, you look positively peaked," she said, shaking her head at me. "Lilias will be fine with me here. Go outside and get some fresh air."

I hesitated. Then Mother smiled at me and nodded toward the door. Next thing, they were gossiping away and I was forgotten. So I left.

I found Tom out in the garden and we were talking when we both caught sight of Father and David coming out of the house together. They did not see us. They looked agitated. We stared across the hollyhocks at them and then, without saying a word to each other, we crept close.

I heard David say, "But I told Nathan I would come over to his house."

"Nathan will survive without you," Father said, not smiling at all. "I want you to come to Roberta Johns's house with me."

"Why?" David blurted. His voice squeaked the way it still does when he is nervous.

I was surprised he dared ask. Usually, when Father says "Jump," we jump.

"You'll see," Father told him. "I have to take some medicine over to Mrs. Forbes on the way. You take the reins."

As they turned to go to the stable, Tom and I didn't even need to ask each other. The minute they disappeared, we broke into a run. Because they had to deliver the medicine first, we actually reached Roberta's ahead of Father.

Luckily, Roberta saw us coming and we had a chance to tell her what was happening.

"Follow me," she whispered, beckoning.

She led us to the big snowball bush next to the house. The parlour window was right above it and it was wide open to catch the breeze.

We crawled into the shelter of its branches. Tom stuck his head out and pulled it back fast.

"They're coming up the walk," he hissed. "Dr. Graham is with them and David looks sick."

We all heard Mrs. Johns greeting them. "Right this way," she said. "The little lad will be nervous at first. He is so afraid someone will make him go back to that beast. It's all right, Jasper. These are your friends. You remember Dr. Cope."

After that, we took turns rising on our toes to peek. David looked snooty at first. Then father showed him Jasper's poor back and his crooked arm and his bones which still stick out. You can count every knob in his spine. The welts and bruises still showed.

"This is dreadful," Dr. Graham growled. It was not a bit like his everyday voice.

"He's red with rage," Roberta whispered.

I looked and saw the veins bulging out in his forehead.

Father said he wanted a witness because, if he hauled Mr. Stone before the law, there were plenty who would stand up and swear the boy was getting his just deserts.

"I know how strong the feeling against these children is running among some of our leading citizens," Dr. Graham said. "It is criminal. I've heard a medical man I won't name say that the boys and girls sent out are diseased in mind and body. The folk at Hazelbrae, and in Toronto, too, protest, but it does little good."

Then he persuaded Jasper to talk about what had happened to him. David looked sicker and sicker as Jasper told about being beaten, left to sleep on the bare floor in the back shed with the dog, given no supper lots of times.

Roberta choked back a sob as Jasper told how he had thrown the dog a bare bone, and when the animal ran to get it, he would steal the mouldy crusts Mr. Stone had put out for it. Jasper said he felt terrible doing this because the dog was starving too, but he could not find any other food. Sometimes, if Mr. Stone went out, his sister would slip him something, but the man seemed to know every time. She was scared of him too. Jasper stole eggs from under the hens, but they were old and skinny and they didn't lay much.

I was glad Sparrow had not come with us. It hurt so to hear him. I can't write any more now. When we got home, I was afraid the baby would have been born while I was gone, but nothing seemed to have changed.

Hurry up, baby.

Bedtime

Here is the rest of what happened at Roberta's.

Dr. Graham offered to report the villain to the police. At his words, Jasper cried out in fear.

"It's all right, boy. We won't do it yet," Father said. His next words astounded me. He told Dr. Graham,

"Billy Grant is growing old. If Lilias and I take this lad in, and he works with Billy an hour or two a day and goes to school with the others the rest of the time, Jasper could take on Billy's job when he gives up. Having Jasper around would make his sister happy as a lark. That little girl has been so good to Lilias."

"If it weren't for her, your Lilias might have lost this baby," Dr. Graham said.

I peeked in again. David was crying. At least, I saw his shoulders shake. When I told Tom, he did not believe it.

Father said he was going to write to the Barnardo people and see about keeping Marianna and Jasper. He even said he would adopt Jasper before he let him go back to that villain.

Then I guess they saw Jasper was exhausted. They came away quietly. David had not said one word. The Johns are going to keep Jasper at their place until Father hears from the Barnardo people.

Tom and I waited until the carriage disappeared and then we came out. We were so full of what we had seen and heard that we hardly said a word to each other on our way home.

Later in the afternoon, Father and Dr. Graham drove out to Mr. Stone's farm without telling anyone they were going. Father told us later that it was run-down and filthy. Mr. Stone was there. There was also a dog skulking around who was nothing but bones.

"I showed the fellow the written report of Jasper's

injuries, and warned him that if he ever came to our home looking for him, I would call the police and give them the report," he said.

Mr. Stone blustered and yelled at them and made threats, but he was one against two and he simmered down. They did not leave until he signed a paper agreeing never again to apply for one of the Home Children.

"I had to be sure nobody else would ever suffer at his hands," Father told Mother.

"But what if the child is permanently injured?" Mother said in a shaking voice.

Father said that children are blessedly resilient. "With careful nursing and good food," he said, "Jasper will be a changed boy by the first of September."

I had not remembered school would start so soon. The thought of Mr. Grigson looking down his nose at Jasper pains my heart. He won't be in our classroom because he is just eight, but Mr. Grigson is the principal and oversees all the children. Tom has passed his Entrance and will not be going with us any longer. Dear Diary, I will confess to you that I will miss him terribly.

I told Father I wished they had saved the starving dog.

"Have a heart, Victoria," Father said. "I cannot right all the wrongs in the world. If it is any comfort, I saw the dog and he will not live long, I fancy. He's nothing but bones."

It was my turn to cry myself to sleep. Snortle tried to comfort me, licking my cheek with his soft tongue. But it made the grief harder to bear. Finally he pushed himself up close against me and went to sleep, snortling gently. He has been cosseted since he was born, while that other dog . . . I can't write any more.

Saturday, August 7

The baby has still not been born. The pains have not started up again. I asked Marianna why and she said it just happens sometimes.

"They'll start up again, don't fret yourself," she said.

We had bread and butter and tea. Marianna made Father eat more but didn't bother me with food. They seem worried. I feel frantic. I had no idea it could take so long.

Sunday, August 8

Nothing happened today. It feels as though we are all walking around holding our breath.

Monday morning, August 9

Her pains came back about ten o'clock last night. I stayed awake all night. I never did that before. Maybe my eyes closed for a few minutes now and again, but I heard our grandfather clock chime every hour.

Mother is moaning. I feel I cannot bear it. But you

don't have a choice. I tried to talk to the doctor, but he just said, "Don't worry, child," as though I were five years old and had no notion what was happening. Of course, I wouldn't know if it weren't for Marianna explaining it all. I was shocked when she did, but I'm glad now. So many girls are told lies about babies coming.

I am writing any old thing to keep from crying. But I'm starting to cry anyway. I can't see to write and the ink is getting blurry with tears.

Oh, baby, do hurry up.

Afternoon

Mrs. Johns came around noon and everything was much better. The doctor listens to her. She seems to know just what to do.

"Don't look so woebegone, Victoria," she said, smiling at me and smoothing my hair. "I've had four and they are all alive and kicking. We'll get this little one safely into the world before long. If she or he was not determined to come wrong way around, it would all be over by this time."

I felt shy but I asked how they usually came.

"Head first," she said. "Diving into the world. But this one is arriving the other way up and giving us a bit of trouble."

It makes me feel queasy to think of it coming out.

I can hear Mother crying out. I am never going to have a baby. Never, never, never.

Monday . . . No, it is Tuesday,
August 10, 2 A.M.

I cannot believe it. I have a little sister! She is very small but she is alive. Marianna says she is NOT small at all for a new baby. Father weighed her even though it was the middle of the night. She weighs seven pounds. She is red and wrinkled and she has hands like a doll's. Yet she can cling to my finger so tightly.

I should be sleepy but I feel as though I will never need to sleep again. Father is excited too. When he came out of the bedroom and told us, he had a huge smile.

"A sister for Victoria Josephine Cope," he said. "Just as you ordered."

I told Marianna that my sister reminds me of a rosebud.

"She's pink but she's no flower," Sparrow said. "She's a person and you just wait. You have no idea how much work a baby can be. Or how they smell."

I would have been angry, but I saw tears in her eyes and remembered she had a little sister too. I don't think I understood how it must hurt her to think of Emily Rose, until I held our baby.

Father took me in to see Mother before I was sent off to bed. She was very white with red patches in the middle of her cheeks. Her hair was loose and damp-looking. But her smile was her very own smile.

"Isn't she lovely, Victoria?" she whispered.

I nodded. If I had tried to speak, I'd have burst into tears.

It is the strangest thing, dear Diary, how you can be so happy and so sad at the very same moment. It is confusing. But it feels right.

I am sleepy after all. Good night.

11 A.M.

When I woke up it was almost ten o'clock! I could not believe it. Father told me Mother was sleeping, so I ate a huge breakfast. I had not felt like eating for days.

Then Mother wakened and I went to see her and my little sister again. Mother told me she wants me to name her. We have talked over names but Mother would never choose. I believe she thought it was bad luck. She just said we should wait until we meet the new person and pick a name that belongs to him or her and nobody else. Now she is trusting ME to do the choosing.

"Not Hepzibah," she said, "but I know you will choose the perfect name."

Then Father said we must leave her to rest.

I have a sister!

Wednesday, August 11

It was so astonishing to wake up and hear a baby crying. It took me a moment to figure out what I was hearing. She sounded a little like a lost kitten. But she doesn't cry much. She SLEEPS!

I tried to settle on a name for her, but it is not so easy. I kept thinking of Marianna's little sister's name. Emily Rose. It seemed to fit our baby, but I thought Marianna would not like us using it. Finally I told her.

She stared at me wide-eyed. Her eyes really did go big and round. Then she gave me a fierce hug.

"My mother would be honoured," she said.

Mother and Father think it is lovely. So Emily Rose is my little sister's official name even though we are all calling her Rosie right now. Well, she is so tiny. Father can hold her in his cupped hands. Not that he does. We have to keep her warm and handle her as though she is made of eggshell.

Father smiled when I told him the name. "I was terrified you'd want to name her Jubilee," he said.

I'm glad she did not wait any longer to be born or she might have been a Wednesday's child. They are "full of woe." Tuesday's child is "full of grace." You can't see it yet, but she will grow graceful in time.

Thursday night, August 12

Marianna was absolutely right. Babies are not rosebuds. They are hard work. We not only have to care for her but be nice to all her visitors — Mrs. Jordan and Cousin Anna, Uncle Peter and Aunt Gwen, Grandma and Grandpa Cope, Mrs. Cameron, the minister.

Mother says, "At a time like this, you have to expect the world and his wife."

I am tired of saying that my nose is not out of joint and that I don't care about not being the baby of the family any longer. I am weary of smiling at them while they go on and on teasing. I love her. I really do.

Good night, dear Diary.

Friday, August 13

Another day crammed full of baby. Snortle is jealous.

Saturday night, August 14

I rocked Rosie to sleep again. She goes to sleep for me every time. She feels so small and warm and darling. But now I need to sleep myself.

Sunday, August 15

The baby is asleep again! Father and the boys went to church but I stayed home to help Marianna. At the moment, Mother and Rosie are both asleep and Sparrow is making some special dish.

"Go away, Victoria," she said, smiling. "I have to think."

I was glad because I was in the mood to write.

Babies are not just sweet. Ours is forever needing to be changed or fed or rocked. All those diapers have to be washed and folded. Marianna irons them! Rosie wakes us up too. She is not a peaceful child. Mother says she will settle down.

I do love her so!

Thursday, August 19

I put my diary down in the hammock and someone took it and I could not find it anywhere. It has finally shown up under my bed. I know I did not leave it there. I suspect Tom. I will skip August 16, 17 and 18. Nothing really exciting happened. Babies don't stay exciting, but they do keep holding onto your heart as tightly as they grip your finger.

Friday, August 20

Today David actually drove over to bring Jasper home. He has been going every so often to visit Lou Johns and he has spent time with Jasper. My big brother seems changed. Not that he is perfect. He called me Picky Vicky tonight when I would not eat my turnips.

The funny thing is, I am certain he hates turnips himself.

Jasper's hair is growing in and is back to its glorious red. His cheeks are rounding out and peppered with golden freckles. His bones don't show any longer and his grin now blazes like sunrise.

Sparrow is as happy as a dog with two tails, having him with her and not needing to hide him. He has a husky voice and he is still a bit shy. He'll be starting school in September. They talked about asking the teacher over to meet him, but it did not happen for some reason.

Mother reads to him when Rosie is asleep. She is still supposed to be resting a lot and the two of them are enjoying sharing Tom's and my old books. When she read to him from *Little Men*, they both cried over Nat, who is like a Barnardo Boy in lots of ways.

Having Jasper in the family has changed other things too. Marianna hovers over him! She hovers over Mother and Rosie too. She hardly has time to talk with me any longer.

I sound jealous. I don't think I am, really. I am just lonely sometimes.

But there is lots to take my mind off myself. We are going to Grandma and Grandpa Cope's later to help with the harvest. David is still mostly with them. When he does come home, he is so quiet he seems like someone else. I cannot believe this, but I miss the old David.

Thursday, August 26

I took my diary downstairs and lost it. Marianna found it this morning under all the baby's washing. I should have missed it terribly, but I am so busy these days that I was a tiny bit thankful not to find it.

But now, dear Diary, I have you back and I will take better care of you.

When Emily Rose grows up and finds this diary, she will want to know what happened on the days I keep missing. Sorry, Rosie. The true answer is "Not much."

I am trying to teach Jasper to read and figure better, before school starts. He looks so odd still. And his arm was too badly broken to be fixed, so he may be teased by some of the boys. But he has me and Roberta to stand up for him.

I found the poem Marianna's mother named her after. We laughed and laughed. Tennyson's Marianna is not like Sparrow at all. She's moping and whining. "A regular watering pot," Tom would call her. And the poem goes on and on and on for PAGES. Sparrow despaired of her and quit halfway through, but I thought it might turn out happily in the end. It didn't.

Men are coming to put in the bathroom as soon as Mother is well enough. They are going to use the little sewing room. There will be a tub with hot and cold water. I can't quite imagine it.

Friday, August 27

Today Marianna Wilson turned thirteen. She says she is a woman. I see no evidence of this.

Happy birthday, Sparrow.

I made her a burnt leather cake and it was not too bad. It fell in the middle but it tasted fine.

Sunday, August 29

After recording Sparrow's birthday, I let another day go by without writing anything. And I vowed to do better. There just never seems to be time. I would be too tired. And Sparrow and I would get talking. Also, looking after a baby is a lot of work.

Snortle is so jealous of the baby! I wonder if he thinks Rosie is a puppy. He goes to Jasper for comforting. Yet when Mother puts Rosie down on a blanket, Snortle approaches her so carefully and just stands and breathes on her.

Everything has felt a bit flat lately. No Jasper to hide! No baby to wait for! No Aunt Lib to set off sparks. I am glad all of that is done but, in a strange way, I miss it. It is so tame to write, over and over again, in my diary, "Picked blackberries."

I liked picking blackberries though. It was peaceful. And I loved looking at Marianna growing happy and Jasper growing healthy. He's happy too. He looks more like the boy I first saw at the railway station, except now he has a permanent grin on his face.

School starts in just two days, so I'll have new adventures to tell you about, dear Diary.

❧

Monday, August 30

Tonight I will have a bath in our own bathtub and let the water run away down a pipe. Amazing!

Now Marianna is thirteen, she asked Mother if she could stop going to school. She says she wants to look after Emily Rose, and I know that is part of the truth. I also know she wants to escape from the jeers of Nellie Bigelow and her kind, all the ones who despise Home Children. There are not many of them, but their taunts and belittling glances sting.

Mother told her she must go half days at least. Then she can bring her work home and Mother will help her.

"You have a good head on your shoulders," she said. "It is best for you to keep on at school, Marianna. And Jasper will need you, I am sure. You owe it to your brother to be there, and I owe it to your mother to do my best for you."

I don't know what she meant exactly.

Then she made Marianna learn the 23rd Psalm to the tune the covenanters made up, and told her to sing it whenever she felt she needed extra strength.

Marianna sings it constantly, putting special emphasis on "A table Thou hast furnished in presence of my foes."

She sings it and sings it. I told her she was as bad as Peggy bawling out "Annie Laurie," but she was not at all crushed.

"Any minute now, I'll clap my hand over your mouth," I told her.

"Put both hands over your ears instead, Picky Vicky," she said.

She is getting too big for her britches — if she wore britches. When she came in May, she would never have spoken to me like that. But we weren't friends then. We are almost like sisters now.

Tuesday, August 31

Tomorrow school starts. I am glad. I groan when anyone mentions it, but secretly I am glad. I have new clothes to wear. A tartan dress with a white collar. I also have a new pencil box.

September

Opening Day,
Wednesday, September 1

Mr. Grigson is gone! Hallelujah!

We have a new teacher. She's a woman named Miss Abbot. She is pretty but tall and strong. None of the boys try to play tricks on her. She walks around with the pointer in her hand and has already cracked it over a couple of their heads. Not hard, of course. But hard enough to get their attention.

We have three new students, besides Jasper, and one of them is a Home Girl. She is twice the size of Marianna, with big shoulders and huge red hands and snapping grey eyes. Her hair is the colour of taffy, but nobody is calling her Taffy, you can bet your bottom dollar.

She is meek as Moses when the teacher is present, but when no adult is around, her true self pops out.

She eyed Nellie up and down and said, "You've never been outside Canada, I suppose. You can't help it. But you have a lot to learn."

"Where've YOU been, pray tell?" Nellie jeered.

"I was born in Dublin. I've lived in Liverpool and in London. I've seen the Queen lots of times," said Molly. "Perhaps you can travel when you grow up."

I was shocked at her sauciness and Marianna's eyes were wide with astonishment. I couldn't believe a Home Girl would talk to Nellie like that. Nellie tried to think of something cutting to say back, but by then Sparrow was laughing right out loud.

"Were you at the Girls' Village or just at Stepney Causeway?" Molly asked, turning her back on Nellie.

They banded together right then and there. Roberta and I go around with them a lot of the time, although certain things are different for them — hardships they have shared and we have not.

Friday, September 3

Jasper is in the other classroom, but we see him at recess time every day. He has made friends with Toby Price, who is a quiet little fellow on top but a tough customer underneath. Nobody bothered them after the first couple of fights. Jasper definitely does not fight fair, but he is so small that everybody cheers him on. And Toby is just as bad.

I thought some of the boys, Jimmy Bigelow especially, might run to the teacher, but he only did it once. She made him give up the rest of recess for tale-bearing.

The four of us girls, Molly, Marianna, Roberta and I, are by far the strongest group in the school now. The others mostly steer clear. Molly is so BIG and she isn't afraid of any of the other girls. She can't read properly and can only do sums where you don't have to carry. She doesn't seem to care a pin.

"I'll learn if it's in me," she said. "I know a lot about surviving without book learning, but I would like to know more."

Miss Abbot asked today if any of us liked writing stories. I put up my hand. She asked if she could see some of my work.

Saturday, September 4

I told Mother about Miss Abbot asking to see my writing.

"That is splendid, Victoria," she said. "What will you show her? Make it your very best."

I thought about it and was surprised at my own answer.

"My best writing is in my diary," I told her.

"Good. Let her see it. But do you think I might read it first?"

It was funny. I used to worry that she'd find it and read it. But when she said that, I realized that I had been wanting to show it to her for a long time. I will give you to her, dear Diary, just before I go to bed.

But now I am remembering some of the things I have written. I can't go back and cross out bits, because she would see them at once. Does she know Father thinks she's like a sailing ship? Did I say she had no sense of humour? Did I tell any of Marianna's secrets which she would mind Mother knowing? I feel slightly sick. I think I had better hand you over right away, dear Diary, before I grow so worried I have to tell her I have changed my mind. I think I will take a holiday from keeping a diary until I get you back again.

Labour Day
Monday night, September 6

We had a holiday from school today. Right after breakfast, Mother gave me back my diary.

"Victoria Cope, you are a born writer," she said.

"I'm afraid you will find some tear stains on a few pages. And you made me laugh out loud — even if I am a serious person. I showed bits to your father and he wants to read it next."

I was so pleased I could not speak a word. I could feel myself blushing.

Tuesday, September 7

Jasper boasted to me that he was sent to the blackboard this morning and he got every sum right. He should. We had been over them enough. Tomorrow I will give my diary to Miss Abbot.

Friday, September 10

I planned not to write anything until Miss Abbot gave me back my diary, but I have to. I'll write this in on loose sheets and copy it in later.

The Barnardo people have written back and given Father and Mother permission to keep both Marianna and Jasper here. Mr. Stone was ordered to send his Barnardo trunk over here and he did not. Jasper wanted Father to forget it, but Father said, "No. You have little enough, my lad. That box is your property. He must account for it."

The police went with him to Mr. Stone's place and found it deserted. The dog had been taken in by the neighbours, Father says. I asked him to find out about it and he smiled at me and said he would try. They found Jasper's trunk in the barn. It had never been opened. The farm itself is going to be seized by the bank for bad debts.

"What will a bank do with a farm?" I asked Father.

"Auction it off to the highest bidder," he said.

The neighbours said Mr. Stone had told them he was heading south.

Father also asked about Emily Rose Wilson, Marianna's sister. The Barnardo people say she has been adopted by a good Canadian family who love her dearly and will see she has the best of everything. They are not at liberty to release any more information about the family, or even tell us where she is. They also said that both parents of the Wilson children were dead.

Marianna cried a little, but I think she had guessed this must be true long ago. I also think our baby is helping to heal her grief. Knowing her sister is well is some comfort.

"There's nothing more you can do, child," Mother said to her. "Pray for God to bless and keep her and hold our little one to your heart. Jasper too needs all the love you can spare."

"Yes, ma'am," Marianna said.

Mother looked at her.

"I think it is time you and Jasper started calling us Aunt Lilias and Uncle Alastair," she said thoughtfully. "We've been through a lot together. I don't feel like 'ma'am' any longer."

Sparrow went red as fire and smiled her crooked smile.

"Yes, ma'am," she said.

But Jasper started in right away. Mostly he calls Mother "Auntie Lily" and Father "Uncle Al," which sounded funny at first but is just right now.

Cousin Anna and Mrs. Jordan came here for supper tonight. Mrs. Jordan drove them over in her buggy.

Mrs. Jordan and Jasper looked at each other. She should have defended him more, but I guess she was too timid. I was going to write "too cowardly," but I was afraid of that man myself and I was never alone with him. She patted Jasper's shoulder and he ducked his head down and went pink. But neither said a word. He is still a Home Boy to her.

Sunday, September 12

Emily Rose Cope was baptized this morning. She was so good. Just sucked her thumb and gurgled all through. One of the other babies yelled his head off and punched the minister on the chin.

Monday, September 13

Miss Abbot told me this morning that she had read my diary. She said she wanted to read it again and she will talk to me about it after she finishes.

"It is a remarkable piece of writing for a girl your

age," she said. "You got me so interested in the story of all that was going on at your house, that I did not pay proper attention to the writing itself."

I did write a poem. I finished it today. At least, I think I did. Every time I am sure it is done and I copy it out in my best writing, I see a word I must change. I'll write it out here and give her the other one. I let Tom read it. I had to try it out on somebody. He stared at me goggle-eyed.

"Vic, it sounds as good as anything in the reader," he said in a hushed voice. "Did Father help you?"

"No," I said. I was angry for a moment, but then I realized he was saying my poem was so good he thought a grown-up must have given me some help. It was a compliment, not an insult. I could feel my face go red right up to my hair.

Now I will copy it onto your pages, dear Diary.

Thanksgiving
By Victoria Josephine Cope

Thank You, God, for the whispering breeze,
For the stately grandeur of lofty trees,
For the tinkling laugh of the rippling stream,
For the face of a child in the midst of a dream.

Thank You, too, for the moon at night
As it blesses the world with its cool, clear light,
For the silent hour at the close of day,
For the soft, warm rain that falls in May.

But thank You most for the eyes I see
That look with such love and pride on me.
For those I can turn to in time of need,
Oh, God, thank You for these indeed.

It took me a long time to write and I still feel it isn't even close to perfect. I could go on and on. I also wanted to put Snortle in and Miss Abbot and Emily Rose and Mother. Well, I did, in a way. I need a better word to describe the stream. "Tumbling" maybe.

Writing poetry is harder work than writing in a diary, and not as much fun as telling a story. But it satisfies me somehow in a way those others don't. I have to work so much harder at it. I can't describe the feeling. Long ago, Father asked me what I thought of the world, and I said it was wonderful.

But many times during the past months I have known it is also a sad world and a dangerous one, a world where people like Cousin Anna can grow up with a mother who doesn't want her, where a person like Marianna and Jasper's mother has to give up her children just because she has not enough money to feed them, a place where girls like Nellie Bigelow can be cruel and not suffer for it. I could make a much longer list. It is not quite the world I thought.

But it is MY world and so I am thankful for everything wonderful that is in it — like my friend Sparrow and my baby sister Emily Rose.

My diary has only a few pages left in it. When I

copy all this in, I believe I will have filled the whole book. I don't see how people make one book last a whole year. My writing is not small and tidy, of course, but most people would not have as much to tell about as I have had.

I was going to ask for another one for Christmas. But I just turned back the covers and I noticed something sticking out from under my pillow. It is a brand new diary with a ribbon to mark my place. And Mother has written in the front:

> *For my beloved daughter,*
> *Victoria Josephine Cope,*
> *who is already a fine writer.*
> *With her mother's love.*

It is not only our Queen who feels like jubilee!

Epilogue

꧁♥꧂

Victoria Cope kept a journal all her life, but she did not become a published writer until she was fifty. She was twenty-four when she married a Presbyterian minister. The pair went to China to serve as missionaries. They had one daughter and four sons. Victoria wrote stories for them which they read and reread. These tales were packed with adventure. Years later her daughter, Marianna Rose, sent the stories off to a publisher, who brought them out in serial form in a children's magazine. Both boys and girls waited eagerly for every issue.

Victoria's children were sent home to Canada to be educated. As she said goodbye to them, she thought with sympathy of Marianna's mother leaving her children at the Barnardo Home. Victoria herself started a small school for orphan girls in China, and became well loved by her pupils. When her husband died, she returned to Canada, to live in a cottage in Guelph. There she told more stories to her spellbound grandchildren.

Marianna Wilson trained as a midwife, and went out west to work in small prairie towns. She was famous for the number of healthy babies she brought into the world. Jasper lived with her until he found a sweetheart who loved his red hair and bright eyes.

Marianna never married. She was engaged to be married at one time, but her fiancé was killed in Flanders during the First World War.

Nor did she and Jasper ever learn the whereabouts of their younger sister. Marianna remained close to Emily Rose Cope, however, and never lost touch with Victoria, even though an ocean separated them.

David did not marry, but Tom did. He and his wife had three girls, of whom he was terribly proud.

Both David and Tom enlisted during World War I. Tom served as a pilot in the Royal Flying Corps and came home without a scratch. David was shell-shocked, however, and had to be hospitalized for months after the war ended. He was never fully well again. His years in the trenches cured him of his narrow-mindedness, but left him permanently disabled. He died when he was just 47, of pneumonia.

Victoria and her husband named their first son David.

Historical Note

❧

How would you like to go back in time? Most of us would say yes at once if we were given the chance. You have imagination and an enquiring mind. Let me send you back.

It is 1897 and you now stand on Drury Lane, in London, England. You are so hungry that you feel faint. You ate the last of the bread you had yesterday noon, and you don't know where you can get more. You are barefoot and it is a cold, rainy November day. You do have a ragged dress and an old shawl, but the icy wind cuts right through them both. Your hair is filthy and you have lice. You also have a sore throat and a bad cough. You feel utterly alone, very ill and in despair.

What can you do? You have no relatives you know of. You could go to the poorhouse, but everyone says never go there. You won't get enough to eat there anyway.

You could try begging, but that takes courage you no longer have. You know of only one other choice. Other homeless children have told you, "You can always go to Barnardo's."

So you make your weary way to London's east end, to the Barnardo Home at Stepney Causeway. If you could read you would be comforted by the sign which says that no child like you will ever be turned away. With a gulp, you march up to the big front door and ask to be let in.

The worst part of being a destitute child is now behind you. They wash you and cut your hair short and give you warm clothes and shoes. They feed you. They wake you early and keep you busy every minute of the day, training you for a job as a servant. They are teaching you to know your Bible and to read. You meet Dr. Thomas Barnardo himself. He is terribly busy, but he smiles at you and he actually remembers your name. He makes you feel you matter to him. It is a long time since you felt you mattered to anyone.

Then you are offered another choice. "How would you like to go to Canada?" they ask.

The Barnardo children who were chosen to go to Canada were told it was their chance to make a fresh start in a new land. Canadian families needed their help. They would be sent to school in Canada if they were younger than twelve. They would be paid for their labour if they were older — although the money would be kept in trust for them until they were set free to go their own way. To most of the children it sounded like an adventure.

"What's Canada like?" they asked each other. Nobody knew, but rumours flew: It was wonderful there. Some who had gone were now rich! Canadian families loved you as though you were their own children.

Life at the Home was regimented and predictable, but life in Canada would offer opportunities undreamed of in England. Most children chose to go eagerly. Some who hesitated were sent along willy-nilly.

Dozens of boys and girls, each with his or her distinctive Barnardo trunk, marched up the gangways onto big ships. Siblings like Marianna and Jasper crossed the Atlantic together, but were often separated once they reached their destination. Many did not realize until they were at the railroad siding in Belleville, east of Toronto, that they would not continue to the same Barnardo Home as their sisters or brothers. This would have been wrenching for children who had already lost their parents.

Girls settling in Ontario were first sent to Hazelbrae, the Barnardo reception home in Peterborough. Boys went to the Home on Peter Street (later moved to Farley Avenue) in Toronto. In fact, Marianna and Jasper's finding each other on the same train to Guelph, after they had originally been separated, was a surprising but happy coincidence.

Where did this idea of sending English children to Canada come from? Why did kind Dr. Barnardo send so many children overseas? Who was he exactly?

Thomas John Barnardo was an intense young man who burned with the desire to be a missionary doctor under the China Inland Mission. Unable to pursue that dream, he turned to working at one of the

Ragged Schools for poor boys.

Then came Jim Jarvis, the boy who changed the direction of Barnardo's life. In a story he wrote himself, Barnardo told of how, one night, when he was shutting up his Ragged School, he found one boy still there after the others had gone. He told the boy it was time he left for home.

"I have no home," Jim Jarvis said. Barnardo asked where his parents lived. The boy said he had none.

"Where did you sleep last night?" the man asked.

The boy took the young man to see where homeless boys slept — under bridges, in alleys, in cramped spaces under the roofs of tenement buildings. Dressed in rags, huddled together for warmth, and gaunt with hunger, they slept on the bare floor. They lived on whatever scraps of food they could beg or steal.

Thomas Barnardo was shocked — and deeply moved. In the following days, he set about providing such children with a place where they would have safety, food and shelter. He eventually opened a home for "waifs and strays" in Stepney, a poor district in East London. (He later founded a Girls' Village Home at Ilford, Barkingside, Essex, and a Babies' Castle in Hawkhurst, as well.) As word spread, so many boys came seeking refuge that one night a boy known as Carrots had to be denied entrance because there was no room for him. Later he was found dead of exposure. Dr. Barnardo was so appalled by this that he decided no child in need would ever be turned away again.

Barnardo kept to his resolve even though it grew harder and harder to find enough money and room to house so many destitute children. Finally he decided to follow the lead of Annie Macpherson and Maria Rye, two women who had already sent children to Canada, where people were crying out for help on their farms.

Some 60,000 Barnardo Children were sent to Canada between 1875 and 1930. For many, the scheme worked. These children settled into their new lives quickly, and grew up to consider themselves Canadians. At least one Home Boy inherited the family farm under the terms of his employer's will. Many of the children, however, were homesick for Britain. They were urban children who had never seen a live cow, never had to gather eggs from under clucking hens, never lived away from the noise of traffic and the press of people. They had accents different from those of Canadian children. Those who had lived by their wits, like today's street children, often were not used to taking orders from adults who were impatient with their lack of knowledge or skill.

Some men and women to whom Home Children were sent were far too harsh, and treated the children badly. Some boys were made to sleep in woodsheds, and fed only scraps. Some girls were abused and, when they sought help, were not believed. There were even a few cases where farmers were convicted of murdering the boys.

Under such conditions, some Home Children responded in anger or tried to run away. If the Barnardo people learned of the treatment, these children might be relocated to other farms or homes, where it was hoped they would be happier. Some youngsters were moved up to ten times! Such heartbreaking stories are painful to read.

The Barnardo inspectors, whose job it was to make sure the placements were safe and happy, made hurried and infrequent visits. The host homes and farms were often far out in the country and the distance to be travelled great. The inspectors also commonly interviewed the children in the presence of the adults — something that would not be done today — so the children might have been too frightened to speak up about any problems. A few who did tell of their misery were even given stern lectures instead of the understanding they deserved.

Bit by bit people saw that the child immigration system was in need of a change. In 1924 the new Labour government in Britain decided that the Home Children, as British subjects, should stay home, at least until they were fourteen. The last child emigration scheme, the Fairbridge Farm School at Duncan on Vancouver Island, ended soon after World War II.

What happened to Home Children in their later lives? Many became domestic servants or farm labourers. Many married and had families of their own. Some never told their children that they had immigrated as Home Children. Others were proud of what they had made of their lives, and shared their stories with all who asked. Some went on with their schooling and became nurses, teachers or doctors. Perhaps one of them was a grandparent of yours, or a great-aunt or great-uncle. Ask the older members of your family and see what you can learn.

❧

My own mother's grandparents took in a Barnardo Boy named Tom, to help Great-Grandpa in the blacksmith shop. Tom had no memory of his surname although he had been assigned one by the Home. Once he settled in, he asked my great-grandfather if he could take his name, since he wanted a name he could be proud of. Great-Grandpa told him he would be honoured, and the boy became Tom Mellis. He grew up to take over the blacksmith shop. Tom's many descendants are known by the name Mellis today.

There are still a few Home Children alive in Canada. I met one Barnardo Girl face to face, just two weeks before her death. Ethel Crane died in 2000 when she was 102 years old. She came to Canada with her brother and sister in 1914. Ethel was one of the unfortunate children who did not know until she reached that Belleville train siding that she and her brother and sister would be separated and sent to different Homes.

Ethel had a hard life, but eventually found her siblings again, and later married. She named her son after her brother, Alfred. She was ill when I met her, but when she told me she clearly remembered Dr. Barnardo, I felt as though I was standing in the presence of history.

"He was a very good man," she said. "Everybody liked him. He cared about us all."

That is not a bad epitaph for Thomas John Barnardo.

BARNARDO GIRL'S CANADIAN OUTFIT IN 1898

new box
label
key
stationery
brush and comb
haberdashery
handkerchief
Bible
Sankey Hymnbook
2 stuffed dresses (blk/gold)
2 print dresses
2 flannelette 'n dresses
2 cotton 'n dresses
garters
shoe and boot laces
toothbrush
8 small towels in bag

2 pair of hoses (thick)
2 pair of hoses (thin)
2 flannelette petticoats
1 winter petticoat
1 summer petticoat
2 coarse flannel aprons
2 holland aprons
2 muslin aprons
ulster
tam o' shanter
hat
1 pair of boots
1 pair oxfords
1 pair slippers
1 pair plimsoles
1 pair of gloves

Haberdashery would be small items such as buttons and needles. An ulster is a long, loose undercoat made of rough cloth. Oxfords are sturdy leather shoes and plimsoles (or plimsolls) are rubber-soled canvas shoes.

Queen Victoria was Britain's longest-reigning monarch, ruling the Empire for sixty-four years, from 1837-1901. Victoria, B.C., is named for her, and Alberta takes its name from her beloved husband, Albert. Queen Victoria's pug dog, May, also had her portrait painted, along with her puppies.

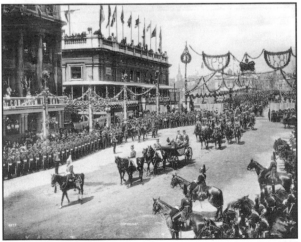

Queen Victoria's Diamond Jubilee procession, on June 22, 1897, in London, England.

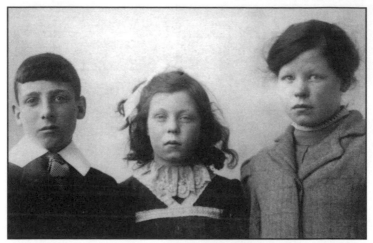

Ethel Parton (right) volunteered to come to Canada as a Home Girl in 1914, with her sister Hilda and brother Alfred. The author was able to interview Ethel before she died in 2000 at the age of 102.

In this 1912 photograph, the widow of Dr. Thomas Barnardo bids a group of Home Girls farewell. They're about to travel on a special train, bound for Liverpool, where they will board a ship destined for Canada.

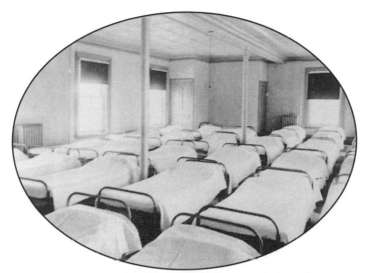

A dormitory room at Hazelbrae, the Barnardo Home for girls, situated in Peterborough, Ontario. Girls stayed here a short time before being placed in Canadian homes.

A classroom at Hazelbrae, with similarly dressed girls learning their lessons.

213

Exterior view of Hazelbrae, a large home given rent-free to the Barnardo charities in 1883 by George A. Cox, Mayor of Peterborough and President of the Midland Railway Company of Canada. The large residence could house up to 150 children, and was the Canadian distribution home for Barnardo Girls between 1868 and 1922.

The house where the story takes place, and where author Jean Little grew up.

A Guelph street scene in the 1870s. Peterborough, where Hazelbrae was located, has a Barnardo Street named after Dr. Thomas John Barnardo.

214

Old Nursery Rhyme

Monday's child is fair of face.
Tuesday's child is full of grace.
Wednesday's child is full of woe.
Thursday's child has far to go.
Friday's child is loving and giving.
Saturday's child works hard for a living.
But the child who is born on the Sabbath Day
Is bonny and blithe and good and gay.

Anonymous

How to Make a Mustard Plaster

Take a piece of old sheeting about 1 foot by 2 feet, depending on the size of the patient's chest.

Mix, in a cup: half a cup of flour, 1 rounded tablespoon of dry mustard powder and one teaspoon of baking soda.

Add water to make a thick paste.

Spread the mixture on half the sheeting. Fold over the other half of sheeting, tucking in the edges.

Apply mustard plaster to bare chest of sufferer for twenty minutes. Take care that the paste does not go directly onto the skin.

Recipe for Burnt Leather Cake

½ Cup Watkins Original Grapeseed Oil
1¼ Cups White Sugar
2 Eggs
1 Teas. Watkins Caramel Extract
1 Teas. Butter Extract
2 Cups All-Purpose Flour
1 Tbsp. Watkins Baking Powder
½ Teas. Salt, if desired
1 Cup Milk
Caramel/Butterscotch Filling and Frosting

Mix oil and sugar, added gradually, beating between additions.
Add eggs, one at a time; beating well after each addition.
Stir in extracts.
Combine flour, baking powder and salt; add alternately with milk, beginning and ending with dry ingredients; blend well.
Pour into 2 greased and floured 8-inch round layer pans.
Bake at 350 degrees F. for 30 to 35 minutes.
Cool in pans; remove from pan; then add filling between layers and frost.

Caramel/Butterscotch Filling and Frosting

2½ Tbsp. Watkins Butterscotch Dessert Mix
½ Cup Brown Sugar
1 Cup Milk
2 Egg Yolks
2 Tbsp. Butter or Margarine
½ Teas. Watkins Caramel Extract
1¾ to 2 Cups Sifted Powdered Sugar
Melt butter in small saucepan; add brown sugar and cook until sugar dissolves (may look curdled).
Stir in milk and extract.
Cool.
Beat in enough powdered sugar to achieve spreading consistency.

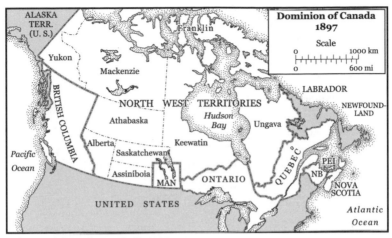

The Dominion of Canada in 1897.

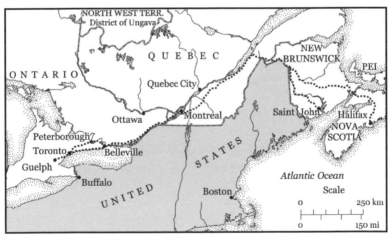

Dotted lines show train routes from places where Home Children disembarked from the ships that had carried them from England to Canada. Near Belleville, girls took a train heading to Hazelbrae in Peterborough, while boys proceeded to the Barnardo Home on Farley Street in Toronto. Many Home Boys travelled farther west to work on farms on the prairies.

Acknowledgments

꧁꧂

Grateful acknowledgment is made for permission to reprint the following:

Cover portrait: W. J. Topley/National Archives of Canada, detail, colourized PA 151708.

Cover background: National Archives of Canada, colourized PA 41785.

Page 210: Courtesy of Woodland Publishing and Gail Corbett, from *Barnardo Children in Canada*.

Page 211 upper: National Archives of Canada C-019313.

Page 211 lower: National Archives of Canada C-028727.

Page 212 upper: Courtesy of Alfred Crane and Kitchener *Record*.

Page 212 lower: Barnardo's Photographic Archive.

Page 213 and page 214 upper: City Archives/Peterborough Centennial Museum and Archives.

Page 214 centre left: Courtesy of author.

Page 214 lower: National Archives of Canada 103121.

Page 215 upper: "Monday's Child": Anonymous.

Page 215 lower: Courtesy of Ailsa Little.

Page 216: © 1999 WATKINS: HEALTHIER LIVING SINCE 1868

Page 217: Maps by Paul Heersink/Paperglyphs. Map data © 2000 Government of Canada with permission from Natural Resources Canada.

Thanks to Barbara Hehner for her careful checking of the manuscript, and to Dr. Joy Parr, author of *Labouring Children*, for her historical expertise.

For Mary Ronzio,
an inspired researcher and cherished friend

About the Author

❧

Orphan at My Door is Jean Little's thirty-first book. She began writing as a child, and, encouraged by her family, has continued writing ever since. Victoria's poem on page 197 was one that Jean wrote when she was only twelve. To date she has written 16 novels and 7 picture books, 3 books of short stories and poetry, and 2 autobiographies — *Stars Come Out Within* and *Little by Little*. She is perhaps best known for *Mama's Going to Buy You a Mockingbird*, *Listen for the Singing*, *Mine for Keeps*, *From Anna*, *His Banner Over Me* and *Hey World, Here I Am!* Such books have won her many prestigious awards, among them the CLA Book of the Year Award; the Ruth Schwartz Award; the Canada Council Children's Literature Prize; the Violet Downey Award; the Little, Brown Canadian Children's Book Award and the Boston Globe–Horn Book Honor Book Award. She received the Vicky Metcalf Award in 1974 for her Body of Work, and is a member of the Order of Canada.

Jean was inspired to write her first novel, *Mine for Keeps,* while teaching at the Guelph Crippled Children's Centre. Sally, the story's heroine, is a real character in every way. How was Jean able to make her so? Perhaps because she can imagine what life is like for a girl with a physical challenge: Whenever you see Jean Little you'll always see a dog, too, because Jean is blind. Her current guide dog, Pippa, has been with her for two years now. Before Pippa, Jean had a black Labrador named Ritz, and before Ritz, a yellow Lab named Zephyr.

How does Jean write her books? She types them into a computer program which then "reads" aloud what she has written. She reads all the time (usually books on tape), even when she's writing one of her own books. Jean says that when she can't read, she can't write.

Readers often remark how true, how real, the people are in Jean Little's books. Characters come to Jean, walk into her mind, and demand to be written about. "My characters are real enough," she says, "that if I get halfway through writing a book and decide I don't want to finish it, what makes me finish it is the characters. Because if I don't finish it, it's like killing them. Their only chance to live is if I finish the book."

Jean's gift is the way she has of listening to those characters, following where they lead, guided by an uncanny knack for creating a story with conflict and drama, and peopled by real characters. She once said, "Your only responsibility as a writer is to be true to the story that has chosen you as its writer."

Jean grew up in Guelph, in the house she has used as the setting for this story. She makes regular visits to schools to meet with fans of her many stories. She tells them that "the best place for your nose is inside a book, so keep reading a Little."

Copyright © 2001 by Jean Little.

All rights reserved. Published by Scholastic Canada Ltd.
SCHOLASTIC and DEAR CANADA and logos are trademarks
and/or registered trademarks of Scholastic Inc.

National Library of Canada Cataloguing in Publication Data

Little, Jean, 1932-
Orphan at my door : the home child diary of Victoria Cope

(Dear Canada)
ISBN 0-439-98834-9

1. Home children (Canadian immigrants) – Juvenile fiction. I. Title.
II. Series.

PS8523.I77O76 2001   jC813'.54   C2001-930337-8
PZ7.L7225Or 2001

The display type was set in Phaistos.
The text type was set in Goudy Old Style.

Printed in Canada
First printing, September 2001

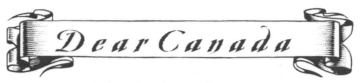
Dear Canada

Other books in the series:

A Prairie as Wide as the Sea
The Immigrant Diary of Ivy Weatherall
by Sarah Ellis

With Nothing But Our Courage
The Loyalist Diary of Mary MacDonald
by Karleen Bradford

Footsteps in the Snow
The Red River Diary of Isobel Scott
by Carol Matas

A Ribbon of Shining Steel
The Railway Diary of Kate Cameron
by Julie Lawson

Whispers of War
The War of 1812 Diary of Susanna Merritt
by Kit Pearson

Alone in an Untamed Land
The Filles du Roi *Diary of Hélène St. Onge*
by Maxine Trottier